THE STORIES OF

EVERGREEN

BOOK III
THE BATTLE FOR GREYSTONE

I0629438

R. S. HAMILTON

The Battle for Greystone

All Rights Reserved

The Stories of Evergreen Book III:

The Battle for Greystone

© 2026 by Venture Creations LLC

Cover design by RebecaCovers

Second edition January 2026

Paperback ISBN: 979-8-9852548-4-6

Please visit us at www.rshamilton.com

VENTURE
Creations LLC

For Lisa,

Thank you for believing in me!

I love you, always and forever!

The Stories of Evergreen Book III: The Battle for Greystone

Billy saw Jared leap his way, but it was much too late. Billy swayed his arms in a circle as he plummeted from the bridge. At first, it seemed to happen in slow motion, but soon things sped up. After a moment, he gave up hope and let gravity take its course. The bridge became smaller and smaller as he fell.

Billy was not scared of death. He had died before, and the result was not all that bad, but he knew this could be the end of everything. What was next? Complete darkness? Heaven? Or a journey to the next world? He didn't know if he had established enough residency in Evergreen to be granted such a journey.

He thought of these things as he fell. There was no fear in him. He plummeted through the mist, and a stream appeared below him. Granite rocks of all different sizes dotted the banks; some were small pebbles, and some were as big as a one-room cabin. As he fell toward one of the big rocks, his last thought was about the book *Jonathan Livingston Seagull* and how Fletcher is forced to swerve into a cliff, only to come out on the other side in a different consciousness.

Billy closed his eyes and wondered what would happen. A moment before he smashed into the rock, he thought to himself, "Jeepers," and darkness overcame him.

Part I: Beginnings

Chapter 1

Every story has a conflict, and every conflict has a history. To understand the history behind the most significant conflict of Evergreen, one would have to go back to the time Raistlin Barrow was born.

Raistlin was born in a small log house on a slope leading down to a barn. Walking further, one would encounter a creek that cut through the green landscape. The landscape behind the home varied from open fields to a hill that led to a rock wall.

Jake and Opal, Raistlin's parents, built the house with the help of Raistlin's grandfather, Randall.

Randall lived alone in a cabin by the river. He became mayor of Ironwood several years before Raistlin's birth and held the office for decades. He was always a man loaded with interesting questions. He was a well-respected man and a well-traveled individual. He was one of the first people to travel to the other world. There was a direct connection through a unique portal. The earliest pioneers of Evergreen were also the architects of this portal. Over the years, the portal sometimes disintegrated, destroyed, or disappeared. Yet, somehow, the portal would be recreated again and again.

Generations later, Lance Erikson would build his version and call it the In Between. It would be a labyrinth of tunnels. These tunnels would lead to portals to the other world but with an extra twist. These portals led not only to different locations but also to different points in time. The In Between also had portals for many activities kids dreamed of doing. Once a child found a portal in their world, they would travel to the In Between and become so immersed in this magical world that they sometimes wouldn't find their way back home. If they ended up stuck in another time, the universe would have the In Between destroyed because traveling time in the other world created a paradox. However, as with the original portal, Lance's magic would build the In Between again. The In Between kept the magic contained within and would continue to grow over time like an expanding universe.

Chapter 2

Raistlin's first word was "Nana"; he said it while stumbling around the kitchen on unsure feet. He and his mother were the only ones there at the time. After a few more times of calling his mother "Nana," the name stuck, and Opal would, from then on, be referred to as Nana. When Raistlin's vocabulary expanded to around twelve words, Dominic and Ginny, who lived just down the hill from Jake and Nana, had a bouncing baby boy. After two days of discussion, they named him Dorn. Unfortunately, before Dorn was able to walk, his mother passed from injuries after falling from a horse that a small porcupine-sized animal called a Hokie spooked as she traversed the edges of the Dark Forest one gloomy evening. Dorn was too young to realize, or ever remember, the loss of his mother. It was a tough loss for his father, but he was always stoic. He mourned in private for quite a long time, but he always stood tall before his friends and son.

Dominic Hale and Jake Barrow worked on building a sawmill near the Snake River, a project that would later benefit the town and its people. Dorn was always there to hand one of the men a wrench or a nail. Raistlin was there occasionally, but he also spent much of his time with his grandfather, Randall.

Raistlin witnessed firsthand the workings of a small town and its people. His grandfather always told him, "We don't want to have to say the 'T word' to our fellow townspeople." He referred to the other world, where people in many places were taxed so their governments could exist. "Taxes can cause wars," he would say.

Instead of relying on taxes paid by citizens, the community of Ironwood would lend a helping hand. When the sheriff's office was built, a handful of carpenters volunteered their time to build the small one-room building. The few businesses in the town were taxed to pay the mayor and the sheriff. Those businesses were the lumber mill, the general store, and the saloon. The smaller proprietors like the barber, the blacksmith, and the cobbler were not taxed. Anyone who made and sold things in their home was not taxed either. A clothes merchant could sell a wagonload of fabric to the general store and not give up a dime of the profits. The idea was to live freely, without much hassle from any authority. It was the concept of Evergreen's pioneers, and thus far, it had worked. Randall Barrow recognized that the community would expand and the town's infrastructure would need to be improved. Perhaps, when that time came, the town government would have to devise a more effective source of income than just taxing the large businesses in town, but for now, the plan in place was working just fine.

Chapter 3

The best kept secret in Ironwood was the dragons that existed. Everyone in Evergreen knew that dragons were at the Barrow homestead, but only a few knew how many there were. There was a cabin north of the Dark Forest that Randall and Jake built before Raistlin was born. There were only two ways to get to the cabin. The easier way was to fly around the Dark Forest on a dragon. A dragon couldn't fly high enough over the thunderstorms constantly raging over the Dark Forest. The other was to trek through the Dark Forest on foot, a difficult task. There was no other way around the Dark Forest besides crossing the river and going through Greystone, which would have been a direct pass by Erikson's Castle. Nobody wanted the headache.

Since Randall spent much of his time in Ironwood, he had an old friend take care of the secluded cabin and train the young dragons. These were the dragons nobody knew about, and the young beasts were watched over and trained. They were too young to fly around the Dark Forest, so their training grounds were on the north side of the forest.

Randall would take Ava, the oldest dragon, and fly to the cabin to check on the young dragons. Often, Jake would come with him.

The dragons were first discovered as eggs in the mountains northwest of the Dark Forest a generation before Randall Barrow was born. They were transported back to camp, and soon, one hatched. Over time, some of the others hatched. There are still a few dragon eggs inside the barn near the cabin up north.

They learned very quickly that the dragons were loyal, friendly creatures. They were trained to hunt and assist with more extensive duties, such as moving fallen trees or picking apples from the highest branches of a tree. They were taught to be on guard and approach strangers with caution. In only a few years, the Barrows and the Hales would cherish the defense training of the dragons. What seemed like a friendly world was about to be corrupted with murder and hate.

Chapter 4

Raistlin and Dorn were close friends when they were old enough to play together. As they grew into childhood, Dorn became a hunter and Raistlin, a gardener.

Dorn often hunted with his father. They hunted everything from pheasant to mule deer. Their prized game was usually too much to feed them, so Dominic shared it with the Barrow family, and they often had feasts together. When it was time for the Day of the Feast, Dominic ensured everyone had plenty of meat.

Raistlin gardened with his mother and father. They grew everything they could and also shared as much food as possible.

These traits of sharing made both families well liked in the community. Many people followed their boilerplate.

The two towns of Evergreen mingled with each other freely to trade, feast together, or enjoy a drink. The only thing that separated them was the Snake River. Years before Raistlin was born, a bridge had been built connecting the two sides. Now, nobody had to ferry across the river on a raft to get to the other town. There was a saloon in each town, and there were often fights. An argument typically started fights between those from opposing towns. The arguments centered on trade, land ownership, or politics. A drunken man from Ironwood often teased someone from Greystone about their taxes. Greystone's citizens were taxed to the point where they couldn't save any money. The tax money went to maintain Erikson's Castle. The citizens of Ironwood were not taxed at all.

After one dreary morning in the fields along the Greystone side of the Snake River, a horrible event brought the conflicts to a fevered pitch. Dorn and his father, Dominic, were hunting on a patch of land that Dominic hoped to purchase. It was dawn, but the sun hadn't yet broken over the horizon.

They both had their arrows nocked, and Dominic whispered to his son.

"They come walking along the riverbank early in the morning." He pointed as he spoke, "They will graze in the tall grass until the sun is bright, then they will hunker down for the day."

Dominic stood for a moment to adjust his position against the tree when he heard a noise behind him. Just as he turned, Ivan Erickson rushed to him and jabbed a dagger into his stomach and upward, piercing his heart. Ivan looked him in the eye as the man slumped toward the ground.

Dorn was dumbfounded. Before he thought to pull his bow back, another man grabbed it from his hands and threw it into the tall grass; then he pushed the boy to the ground. Dorn immediately jumped to his feet and lunged toward Ivan, but the other man stopped him.

Ivan held out the knife, the blade stained with crimson. The same color stained the front of Dominic's green hunting jacket as he lay dead on the ground. Ivan said, "Run! Go back and tell them what you saw!"

So, Dorn ran. He ran with all of his might. He forgot about his bow and arrow; he forgot about everything. The world blurred before him as tears filled his eyes and streaked down his cheeks. He made his way across the bridge, the mist in the air mixed with the tears on his face. He ran through Ironwood. Little pebbles kicked out behind him with every step.

Creed Thompson, the young sheriff of Ironwood, stood on the porch of the sheriff's office sipping coffee when he saw Dorn running down the stone street.

"Dorn? Where you running to, son?" He said. Then, when he noticed that Dorn was bawling, he said, "Dorn? What's the matter?"

Dorn never glanced at the sheriff; he just kept running. The sheriff called after him when he passed, but the boy never looked back. He took the road out of town that led to the Barrow Homestead. He ran right by Raistlin, who was working in the garden.

"Dorn?" Raislin said as he went by.

Dorn burst through the door to Raistlin's house. Nana sat at the table while Jake and Randall looked over a map they had drawn up of the terrain surrounding the Dark Forest. When the door opened, they all looked up.

"Ivan Erikson killed my daddy!" Dorn sobbed.

Jake stood up, "What?"

"My daddy is dead!"

Jake ran to him and held him by the shoulders, "Where?"

"In the field on the other side of the river. We were hunting."

"Go to Nana," Jake whispered and ran out the door.

"Raistlin, unhitch the horses," Jake yelled.

Knowing something was wrong, Raistlin dropped everything and ran down to the barn. Jake began to follow him when Creed Thompson quickly approached the house on his horse. His wide brimmed sheriff's hat hung behind his head with the strap around his neck.

"Jake, what's going on?" Creed said.

Jake stopped and turned, "Dominic Hale has been murdered. In the field across the river. Meet us there."

Once they saddled the horses, Jake and Randall raced toward town. Randall's white hair bounced on his shoulders as they went.

Dorn stood on the porch and watched them go.

Chapter 5

"I'm going to kill the son of a bitch!" Jake yelled.

He was putting on his leather vest over a white shirt. Leather chaps covered his trousers. He strapped a dagger to his belt and put another inside his vest.

"No, you are not!" Nana said, walking to him and looking at him in the face.

"Step aside, my dear," Jake said as he buttoned his vest.

"I won't budge," she whispered.

Nana was as tough as they came. She could chop wood, skin a deer, tan leather, make garments out of animal skins, roast a pig, and whatever else it took to provide for her family and friends. She was the matriarch of the family. She and Jake always made decisions together, but once in a while, she had to stand her ground in a disagreement. This was one of those times.

They stood face to face. He was only a few inches taller than she.

"Jake."

Jake looked at his father sitting in a chair with Dorn sleeping on his lap. Randall shifted to look at Jake and adjusted the boy's legs without waking him.

"You cannot go, Son," Randall said. "As your father and the mayor of Ironwood, I beg you not to go. It is not worth it. Retaliation will start a battle of epic proportions." Randall looked out the window and said, "If I felt it was worth it, I would resign as mayor immediately and let you go." Then he looked back at Jake, "Please, do not go."

Jake thought for a moment, then said, "Yes, Father." He looked down at the floor as his mouth twitched into a frown.

Nana pulled him in for a hug, and he sobbed on her shoulder at the loss of his best friend.

Chapter 6

Raistlin helped his father build a wooden casket for Dominic. When they reached the base of Rickenback Mountain with many of the townspeople in tow, it was Raistlin's turn to cry. As four men lowered the casket into the ground with straps, Raistlin sobbed uncontrollably. He cried until he was about to throw up. Nana wrapped her arms around him and held him tight as the men shoveled dirt onto Dominic Hale's casket.

Dorn stood stoic, just as he would for the rest of his life. A tear streaked down his face, but his eyes were cold, and his jaw was clenched.

Raistlin was nine years old. Dorn was seven.

Chapter 7

Although both towns continued to mingle on the other side of the river, tensions grew in the months after Dominic's murder. There were more fights in the saloons, and trading or bartering something on the opposite side of the river seemed impossible. One side never wanted to give the other side a good deal. Those who were most in need seemed to be those who ended up with the short end of the stick at the close of a deal because the other side could sense their desperation. There were no more set prices or standards. It became a cutthroat world, which was unusual for Evergreen. The harmony was disappearing.

Chapter 8

The months and years that followed allowed Dorn and Raistlin to become closer than ever. They spent most of their days together and every night together since Dorn lived under the Barrow roof. The house Dorn had lived in until his father died sat vacant, although it was well-maintained and used occasionally when someone needed to stay for the night. There were many days when Randall would take Raistlin to town, and Jake would take Dorn to do something. Although Jake was not typically a hunter, he often took Dorn hunting. Two families had worked in tandem, with their hunting and farming responsibilities divided. But suddenly, the hunting side of the deal was gone since Dominic had died. The only way to fill the void was to go hunting themselves. Jake did what he could to help Dorn grow into a great hunter, just as Dominic Hale would have.

Raistlin and Dorn would occasionally walk to town on their own, whether to grab a bag of candy or pick something up for Randall, Jake, or Nana. When he went to town, Dorn always looked for Ivan Erickson; the boys were forbidden from crossing the river to Greystone. Since Ivan had never crossed the river even before he murdered Dorn's father, now he wouldn't even leave his castle grounds. So, Dorn never saw him in town, and Dorn wouldn't see Ivan until decades later when he would visit him on his deathbed.

As they grew into their early teens, they began to see a boy just a few years younger than Dorn playing with his friends on the bridge. The boy was the leader of the group and taller than the others. He would boast and irritate anyone he could. He led the activities with his friends as an act of annoyance to the people in Ironwood.

While speaking with their friend, Zed, at the river bank one day while the boy and his cronies played on the bridge, Raistlin asked, "Who is that boy? The one leading his friends?"

"That's Lance Erickson," Zed said, then he gave a nervous look when he realized he had spoken the boy's name in front of Dorn.

Dorn cooly looked up at the bridge and watched Lance for a few moments; then, he looked down at the river water flowing by. When he looked back up, Lance was watching him. Lance scoffed, turned away, and commanded his friends to follow.

"I'm sorry about that, Dorn," Zed said.

Dorn looked at him and said, "Sorry for what?"

Zed opened his mouth to speak, then closed it as if he thought twice about saying anything.

"What's he like?" Dorn asked.

"Seems like a jerk to me," Zed said, looking up at the empty bridge. "I hear he is already learning his way with the sword."

"Is that so?" Dorn said.

Zed shrugged his shoulders.

#

Two months later, Raistlin, Dorn, and Zed were fishing off the bridge, but they were closer to the Ironwood side of the span. They had been getting skunked all morning and were ready to call it quits when Lance and his ignoramus friends walked up the bridge's approach. Dorn had already pulled his line up, which only had a scrap of a worm left on the hook. He began wrapping the line around the bamboo pole, ignoring the approaching Lance Erickson.

When Lance was close enough, he kicked the tin can the boys used to hold their bait. The can rolled, and wet dirt and worms spilled onto the wooden bridge. Lance's friends laughed like loud drunks in a saloon. Dorn glanced down at the worms, then raised his eyes to Lance. Lance stood above him with a smirk on his face.

Dorn set his pole on the deck and gathered the worms and the dirt in his hands.

Lance turned his head and whispered to his friends, "He's going to go home and tell his daddy about this." He whispered loud enough that Dorn would hear it.

Dorn did hear it, but he kept his cool. He had the worms and dirt in both hands and turned toward the edge of the bridge. He shifted the goods into one hand and went to toss it all into the river but then stopped. He turned to Lance, raised his hand over his head, and dumped the worms and dirt on Lance's head; he had a smirk on his face the entire time.

One of Lance's cronies let out a loud laugh but was cut short by an elbow to the ribs from the boy next to him.

Lance's nostrils flared, and he swiped the worms off his head. He looked at his dirty hand and then pushed Dorn with both arms. Dorn took a step back and then stepped forward and pushed Lance. Lance swiped Dorn's arms away and put up his fists to fight.

Zed was on his feet by this time with his hands balled into fists, ready to fight anyone who dared to join.

Raistlin jumped between Lance and Dorn and pushed them apart. "It's best you get back to Ironwood," he said as he looked at Lance.

"That's okay, I'm not scared," Lance said. "My daddy taught me not to be scared."

Raistlin put his hand against Lance's chest, "Just go home."

Zed jumped forward at Lance's followers, taunting them. They all backed away. In a moment, Lance and his lot were walking off the bridge.

"I could have taken him," Dorn said as they walked off their end of the bridge.

"It's not about who wins," Raistlin said.

"Then what's it about?" Dorn asked.

"It's okay to walk away," Raistlin said.

"Of course it is," Dorn said, but Zed spoke up before he could say more.

"That kid can use a black eye and a busted lip, Raistlin," Zed said.

Raistlin turned to Zed and said, "And what will that prove?"

"It will prove whose toughest."

Raistlin shook his head.

"Look, y'all," Zed said. "I'm glad there was no fightin', but a good crack in the jaw never hurt anyone." He looked around for a moment, then continued, "I gotta get bustin' home. If I don't work the hounds before my daddy gets home, I'm gonna get the switch." He began to walk off. "So long, fellas."

Zed left Raistlin and Dorn standing in the middle of town.

Chapter 9

The tension between Lance and Dorn grew over the next few years. Gossip and rumors grew rampant, but they were all based on one thing: Lance's father had murdered Dorn's father. A fight of epic proportions was brewing, a lifelong tension that would plague the lives of both youths.

The first woman to walk into Dorn's life was Molly. She showed up in Ironwood one day with her father. They both stood in the middle of town with confused looks, as if they had no idea where they were. She was young and wrapped her arms around her father's leg as they looked around the small town. Creed Thompson noticed their unease and came out to help them. They stayed in a room above the saloon for the first few evenings. Then they shacked up with a family that lived by the river. The father and daughter both had nightmares about their transition to Evergreen. They woke up screaming at night with visions of a collision in their previous life, a collision of two vehicles that transported the father and daughter from one world to another.

The only thing that mattered was the tension that brewed over the years. It wasn't a quarrel over a girl. Lance was an expert at digging at a person, and he worked every angle he could to get under the skin of his enemies. He even did it to the people that he thought were his friends. He was a narcissist and a jerk. The fact that everyone knew that his father had murdered the father of a young man in Ironwood fueled his arrogant behavior. He felt as though he was already a king of sorts.

#

Dorn and Molly began courting when they were both seventeen. He was fascinated to hear about her previous life. He knew others who recollected their time before Evergreen and always enjoyed hearing even the smallest tidbit about their existence in another world.

When Dorn wasn't learning the ways of the lumber mill with Raistlin or hunting with Jake, he was helping on the Barrow Homestead. He was an orphan, and the Barrows were his guardians. He did whatever was needed to support the family with their duties. He would often work well after dark to finish a chore.

The house he spent the beginning of his childhood in would soon be his when he felt responsible enough to live on his own. He checked on it often to ensure mice weren't invading or the roof wasn't leaking.

He took care of these things with a vengeance so he would have spare time to spend with Molly. While he spent time with her, Raistlin spent time with Tessa, a girl raised in Evergreen. If they spent time together as a group, Zed and Sally, a girl from town, often tagged along. Zed and Sally had been friends since they were little, and Sally was always interested in how Zed's family raised hounds. Her dream was to raise and breed her own dogs. Surprisingly, Zed and Sally never had a romantic relationship. Zed never showed much interest in girls and never married. Sally looked at Zed as a brother, but she was overwhelmed with jealousy when Dorn started dating Molly. Sally held a crush on Dorn Hale since they were kids. She had high hopes that he would court her one day. Her jealousy subsided when she got to know Molly, and they became great friends.

Chapter 10

An incident on the bridge one afternoon changed the trajectory of the relationship between Ironwood and Greystone forever. Dorn, Molly, Raistlin, Tessa, Zed, and Sally had returned from a horseback ride to Rickenback Mountain. They hitched their horses to the rings on the posts in front of the saloon. Sally's mother owned the saloon, so they all stopped for jerky and colas. Soon, they were back out in the sunlight, strolling through the center of town, leaving their horses for later. They walked their way to the bridge, laughing and joking.

They saw Lance and his friends across the bridge when they walked up the approach. A few of the boys had fishing poles angled over the parapet, their fishing lines leaning away from them in the slow current. Lance was kicking rocks up the shallow slope of the bridge. His friends did the same, trying to mimic his movements without being too obvious.

When Raistlin saw Lance and company on the bridge, he turned to the others and pointed to the shore. "You all want to go down there?" he asked.

Dorn looked at him and shook his head. He knew Raistlin was trying to avoid a conflict. Once Zed realized what was happening, he led the way across the span.

Once Lance realized who was walking across the bridge, he stopped his game of kicking rocks. His friends followed suit. He leaned against the parapet and watched the other group approach.

Zed watched Lance like a hawk while the others conversed as they walked.

Lance began kicking rocks again; his followers followed suit. They walked toward the middle of the bridge, kicking their rocks as they went. As the groups got closer and closer, they both slowed down. The chatting from the Ironwood group quieted. The stones from the other side stayed still on the bridge, but Lance stepped forward and quickly kicked his rock. It promptly took flight and hit Molly in the ear. She yelled and grabbed her ear in pain.

Commotion erupted. Pushing, shoving, and yelling stirred up a cloud of dust. Tessa immediately put an arm around Molly and walked her back to town, leaving the chaos behind.

Lance smiled while Raistlin and Sally tried to hold Dorn back. Zed leaped forward with his fists clenched. He walked to Lance, but one of Lance's cronies stepped forward. The boy put his hands out to push Zed, but Zed landed a punch square on his nose. The boy screamed in pain as he put his hands to his face. Blood began seeping through his fingers. Another boy stepped forward, and Zed threw him to the ground. Dorn pushed Raistlin to the side, but Sally held her hand on Dorn's chest. Dorn would fight his best friend if needed, but he would never push a woman's hand off him. Lance stared at Dorn; the others in Lance's group remained at bay.

"I didn't think hitting her with a rock would hurt," Lance said. "It looks like she has already been beaten with an ugly stick."

Although Dorn stood cool after the comment, Zed rushed forward again. Raistlin reached out a hand and stopped him. Dorn stepped forward, but Sally pushed her hand harder against his chest and whispered, "Don't do this. Please. He is not worth it."

"We're going to end this," Dorn said to Lance.

Lance grinned at him and said, "This ended for me a long time ago. Unfortunately, my friend, this will never end for you."

Chapter 11

Raistlin put his hand on Dorn's chest and stopped him as they walked in front of the sheriff's office. "You can't fight him," Raistlin said. "It won't prove anything."

"It's not about proving anything," Dorn stepped forward and stood facing Raistlin. "This has been brewing for a long time."

"You're trying to fight the wrong person," Raistlin said.

Dorn stepped closer to his friend. "You don't have the right to judge if this is right or not," he said through gritted teeth.

The three women stood to the side; Molly wiped tears from her eyes. Once Dorn stepped closer to Raistlin, Sally stepped forward.

"C'mon, guys," she said. "You are lifelong friends. Don't fight about this."

Dorn turned and looked at Zed. "Go across the bridge, set up a date and time." Dorn looked at Raistlin, then back at Zed, "I will fight him in the middle of the bridge. Nobody else is allowed on the bridge when we fight. Nobody is allowed to step in and break it up. No weapons."

Zed stood with his chest out and his hands in fists, "Whatever you want, my friend."

Dorn paused for a moment, then added, "Bring Fitz with you in case there is trouble."

Zed nodded and walked off.

#

By the time the day of the fight arrived, both towns were aware of the event that was about to take place. Crowds gathered early in the day. Some groups were quiet, while others were loud and confident.

The saloons on both sides of the river opened early, knowing profits were to be made. By the time the sun reached the middle of the sky, many people in each town were drunk.

Jake and Randall Barrow were not in that group. They stood at the stone crossroad of town with Dorn and Raistlin. Tessa, Molly, and Sally stood with them.

Jake put his hands on Dorn's shoulders and looked at him. "So, this is what you want?" he asked.

Dorn nodded. Typically, he wore a leather vest with a cotton shirt underneath. On this day, he was sleeveless. His leather vest matched with a pair of leather pants. He wore no belt nor a necklace of any sort.

"You know I am not in agreement with this," Jake said.

"I understand, sir," Dorn said. "I mean no disrespect." Dorn noticed that Jake had a steer horn hanging from his belt.

Jake took his hands from Dorn's shoulders and said, "I suppose this is what your daddy would want. He was feisty." He glanced at the river for a moment, then continued, "I suppose if he knew what kind of rift was caused by everything that happened, maybe he would have done things differently. He knew he was ruffling feathers when he was trying to get that land, but he never thought it would get him killed. Had he known it would come to this, he would have backed down in a heartbeat." He looked back at Dorn. "But, here we are. If this is how it must be, then I want you to get the best of this guy. Lean into your punches, and remember, defending is just as important as attacking. Protect yourself and wear him down."

"Yes, sir."

#

Minutes later, Lance and his group approached the other side of the bridge. Several people were already lined up at the other bank, but now many more had arrived. People from the Ironwood side began to line the banks; the saloon emptied, and people staggered into the street.

Lance slipped his long coat off his shoulders, obviously wearing it only for show since the day was much too warm to be wearing such garb. He chatted with his friends for a moment, and they patted him on the back and offered words of encouragement.

On the other side, Raistlin paced and ran his fingers through his hair. Of anyone in all of Evergreen, Raistlin was the person who wanted to see this fight the least. He felt that sword fighting and grappling were good for sport, but he vehemently opposed violence against another person.

Dorn and Lance stood at the base of their respective sides of the bridge. The onlookers began to yell across the river at each other. Fists were raised in the air, and a person from Greystone threw a rock toward the other side. It fell far short of reaching the other shore but drew anger from the Ironwood side. The yelling grew louder, and some people from each side began to walk closer to the bridge.

A day earlier, a small group from each town met in the middle of the bridge for a meeting. The rules of engagement were established. There were to be no weapons on either of the fighters. Nobody was to interfere with the fight unless the situation was dire. They would do whatever they could to avoid a fatality.

These two groups were tasked with holding anyone back from crossing the bridge. This was a fight between two young men; nobody else was to join or pick a fight with anyone else.

As the yelling grew louder, a few citizens from each side began to walk up the bridge's approach, but they were held back by the peacekeepers who had been trained the day before.

Dorn started his trek to the middle of the bridge first. He walked with his hands balled into fists. His arms were tan and fit. His leather pants were tight on his legs. His leather boots kicked up dust as he walked. His hair was dark and short, and his eyes were just as dark and fierce. He clenched his jaw as he walked.

Once Lance noticed Dorn walking, he began the trip himself. He also wore leather pants, but he wore a long-sleeved cotton shirt instead of a leather vest. His hair fell to his shoulders, and he held a smirk on his face. His typical bracelets and necklaces were left behind, but he did wear a small loop earring on his left ear.

Once everyone realized the two were approaching each other, the yelling stopped, and all grew quiet. Only the sounds of their boots on the gravel and the birds in the trees along the riverbanks could be heard.

They reached the exact midspan of the bridge at the same time. Pleasantries were strewn aside, and punches were immediately thrown. Before Dorn put his fists up, Lance's lanky arms landed three quick jabs to his face: a right, a left, and another right. Lance's cronies had a good laugh.

Dorn had underestimated the speed of an actual fight. This was different than the usual sparring he had done with his friends in the past. The three punches didn't have much force behind them and only knocked Dorn off balance for a moment. Dorn set his feet and threw a haymaker, from which Lance quickly ducked away.

They both regained their footing and sized each other up. They circled, waiting for the other to make a move. Lance was the aggressor again, throwing a punch meant for Dorn's jaw. Dorn moved forward and took the blow to the back of his head, then returned the favor with four quick punches to Lance's ribcage. He immediately jumped back as Lance hunched in pain for a moment. Then, they returned to their defensive stances.

A punch was thrown by one, then they circled, and another punch was thrown by the other. Dorn grew tired of the waltz, grabbed Lance's shirt, and threw him to the ground. He quickly jumped on top of him and put his knee on his chest. He unloaded half a dozen punches to Lance's face, bloodying his nose and putting a small cut under his left eye.

Lance was surprised at the takedown, and after several blows, he kicked his legs up and pushed Dorn off him. Dorn rolled to the side, and soon, they were on their feet again. Now, the circling and guessing was over. They unloaded a barrage of punches. They stood toe to toe and blasted each other with jabs and hooks. Jake's advice to Dorn about protecting himself went by the wayside. He opened himself to punches but returned them quickly.

Soon, both men had bloodied faces, their clothes were filthy, and Lance's cotton shirt was torn in many places. As the punches' paces increased, the bystanders' sound grew louder. Each side was cheering for their hero. It was a fight that would be talked about for generations.

The pair went back and forth from boxing to grappling on the ground and back on their feet. During the grappling, Dorn ripped Lance's earring from his earlobe. Blood dripped onto his shirt. It was an epic fight. They exhausted themselves and would lean on each other until one of them found a second wind; then, they would go at it again.

At one point, Lance wrapped his arms around Dorn and drove forward. The momentum drove them to the knee high parapet, and they tumbled over the side of the bridge and into the river below.

The Snake River is small, and the depth in the center is about chest high for most people. If one stood in a skiff, they would barely be able to reach the bottom side of the bridge.

Once the pair splashed into the water, they began to pound each other with punches. Their faces were swollen, and the blood seeping from their wounds was diluted by the river water.

The sound of the bystanders grew to a new level once the fighters splashed into the water. The peacemakers forgot about their duties, raced to the parapets, and watched the fighters in the water below. People from each side walked onto the bridge; some of them cheered at the fighters, and others pointed fingers and yelled at the people approaching from the other side. Those on the river banks began to shout and raise their fists at those on the other bank. When Dorn wrapped an arm around Lance and pulled him under the surface, people began to wade into the water, yelling and pointing.

They came up above the surface and gasped for breath, and for a few moments, the fighting stopped. Nonetheless, the bystanders carried on, and their hatred for those on the other side grew.

Chapter 12

Jake and Randall stood side by side, watching the fight and the commotion that was brewing. Once people started creeping toward each other on the bridge and wading into the river, Jake slowly pulled the horn from his belt and held it to his mouth. Because of the sounds of people yelling, only those closest to Jake heard the baritone sound that the horn gave. Only Randall knew what would happen after he blew the horn.

Chapter 13

Both men stood waist deep in the river. Their faces were puffy; their eyes nearly swollen shut. The mob behind each man continued to approach with yells and curses. The fighters grabbed each other and grappled briefly; then Dorn pushed Lance away. The water around his legs helped Lance stay on his feet. He lunged back at Dorn but was met with a haymaker to the jaw. The punch tossed Lance onto his back in the water. Dorn jumped forward, put his hands around Lance's neck, and held him underwater. Once Lance was underwater for a few moments, the crowd on the Greystone side grew to a frenzy. Those that were already in the water began to wade toward the fight.

Dorn held Lance under the water with his hands wrapped around his neck. Dorn began to sob as he choked his enemy. Bubbles came from Lance's mouth and went to the surface. Lance scratched and clawed at Dorn as he was held below the surface. Spittle came from Dorn's mouth as he held Lance underwater. Dorn was in a moment of anger at a level that he would never see for the rest of his life. Once he realized that he was moments away from killing Lance, he pulled him out of the water by the neck and tossed him toward the shore.

Lance made his way to his feet, then staggered backward, trying to catch his breath.

"Don't ever come back," Dorn screamed at him. Due to the commotion, most people on the banks could not hear what he was saying. "If you do, I will kill you! Then I will kill your father, once and for all!"

Lance began to say something but then looked over and past Dorn's head. Just as Dorn started to turn his head to see what Lance was looking at, he heard the huff of one of the dragons.

#

The mobs on each side of the river slowed their approach. They yelled and pointed, taking baby steps as they taunted the other side. When the dragons, called up from the sound of Jake's horn, appeared in the sky, the people from Greystone froze. Donte dropped down and landed on the midspan of the bridge, and Celeste landed on the parapet. They both lowered their heads and roared at the people from Greystone. Chaos ensued. None of the residents of Greystone had ever seen a dragon, and it was apparent the beasts were focused on them. A scramble for the town began. Those in the water started to run to the shore, many falling into the river. Those who were on land or the bridge ran and screamed.

Those on the Ironwood side knew about the dragons that the Barrow family had discovered generations ago, but most had never seen one. They were initially taken aback, but they watched in awe when they realized the dragons were defending their town.

Soon, the other side of the river was clear; everyone had fled back to Greystone.

Dorn waded out of the water, and Molly was the first to meet him. She looked at the wounds on his face, then kissed him on the lips. The others were right behind her. Raistlin, Tessa, Jake, Nana, Randall, Sally, and Zed.

Zed approached him, "It took everything I had not to jump in that fight and help you out."

Dorn nodded.

Sally approached next. She stood before him without saying a word; then she hugged him.

Molly watched the exchange.

Raistlin was still pacing even though the fight was over. He walked to Dorn, patted him on the shoulder, and nodded. Dorn nodded back.

Nana was next. She walked to Dorn and looked at the wounds on his face. His eyes were nearly swollen shut, he had many cuts that needed to be tended to, and scratches adorned his neck. The stitching on his leather vest was torn in many places, and his knuckles were cut and bruised.

"Now you listen to me, young man," she said as she looked up at him.

Dorn straightened up.

"You've gotten this out of your system," she put her hand on the side of his face for a moment. "This has been brewing for a long time; now you need to live your life." She put her arms around his neck, not worrying about any blood she might get on herself or her clothes. "I love you like you are my son. I will love you until the end of our days. Don't you ever forget that. Your daddy would have been proud of you today."

Dorn sobbed for a few moments. His tears created clean paths on his blood stained face. Soon, he regained his composure.

"Now, let's get you home," Nana said. "We have to take care of those wounds."

Randall stepped forward and leaned down to Nana. His long gray hair fell forward, "Can we clean him up at the saloon? The town needs him there."

"Fair enough," Nana said. "To the saloon."

#

Nana found ingredients in the kitchen to make a salve to put on the cuts. She cleaned him up and bandaged his wounds. They all sat at a big table, and Randall turned to Dorn and asked, "What would you like from the bar?"

"I'd like to try whiskey," Dorn said.

"A whiskey for the fighter," Randall said. "And whatever everyone else wants. My tab."

The evening went on. Despite no clear winner, many people came by to congratulate Dorn on the fight. Some tapped him on the shoulder in respect of what he had done. Zed went on and on about different aspects of the fight, replaying some of the moments in front of those at his table. Dorn tried to smile, but even that was painful with his swollen face.

Two things happened that day. Dorn got drunk for the first time, and he gained the entire town's respect. The fight would be talked about for years, but Dorn would always be humble enough to avoid those conversations.

When he woke the following day, he was having trouble breathing. He got out of bed and made his way to the kitchen. He hunched over while he walked. Once in the kitchen, he looked at Nana and said, "It hurts to breathe."

He never took his vest off when he was getting his wounds tended to the night before. Now he stood in the kitchen bare chested. He was bruised and black and blue all around his ribcage.

"Let's get you back into bed," Nana said once she saw the bruises. "We will bring your breakfast."

She applied salve to the bruises. Dorn winced at every touch. Jake and Randall stood in the doorway and watched.

"He will need something to help him sleep," Nana said.

Jake nodded and left the room.

#

Dorn slept on and off for three days before he made his way back to the breakfast table. He winced with every move, but the swelling on his face was down. Black and blue bruises lingered, some fading to a greenish yellow.

They ate silently until Dorn said, "I plan to marry Molly."

Raistlin, Nana, Jake, and Randall all stopped chewing and looked at Dorn.

"I mean it," Dorn said. "Nana told me that I need to live my life. This is the life I want to live. I want to marry her, and I'd like to live in my father's house."

Jake finished chewing and said, "So, it shall be done. If Molly agrees to it, you will be married during the next Day of the Feast."

Smiles and laughter filled the cabin during the remainder of breakfast.

Chapter 14

Dorn and Molly were married during the Day of the Feast, which was always the day the Dragon Moon was full. Marriages were rarely announced before the ceremony. Typically, only the immediate families involved were aware of the upcoming union. So, the townspeople who came to the gathering were pleasantly surprised when Dorn and Molly held hands at the campfire. Randall walked to the couple. Many people began to clap and cheer, knowing what was to come. Randall spoke to the couple, but his voice was too low for most to hear. Finally, the couple kissed, and Randall spoke loudly to the crowd, "Ladies and Gentlemen of Ironwood, I present to you, Mr. and Mrs. Dorn Hale." One full moon later, Raistlin and Tessa were married.

Unfortunately, within a year, Dorn's wife and his unborn child died while she was giving birth. Dorn's unborn child would forever be remembered as Baby Hale and was buried at the foot of Rickenback Mountain, along with his mother.

For some, the culmination of events in Dorn's life would lead to insanity. But Dorn always stayed calm and cool. He would spend the rest of his years in happiness despite the tragic losses in his life. Even though he remained calm, he still held a bit of anger. He loved everyone he was around, but there were two people in his life that he hoped to kill one day. Those people were Lance Erikson and Ivan Erickson. Dorn didn't dwell and seethe over the hatred for these two men; he just held it in the back of his mind—a "to-do" list of sorts.

While Dorn was still mourning his loss, Tessa gave birth to a baby girl. They named her Cambria.

In the first few days of Cambria's life, the sight of her sent pains through Dorn's heart. Soon enough, he adored the baby and held her after dinner every night.

#

Sally's father retired from running the saloon in Ironwood, so Sally took over. She also took over the blacksmith shop after the tenant left town.

Dorn and Raistlin helped Sally remodel the saloon. All of the doors, including the entrance ones and those leading to the kitchen, needed to be fixed. Once they had finished fixing them, they decided it would be best to replace all of them. They resurfaced the bar and replaced many of the wooden stools and chairs. Everything was built or replaced at the mill and then transported to the saloon. The remodel took many moons, but the business remained open.

Now that the towns kept to their side of the river, there were far fewer fist fights in the saloon and the streets. The occasional disagreement happened when a few patrons had too many, and Sally was just as tough during those fights as her father was when he ran the saloon. Her toughness in keeping control of the saloon earned her a significant amount of respect from the townspeople. Many men attempted to court her, but she always denied them. She had eyes for only one man in town, but she would wait for him to mourn his deceased wife and child. She didn't care how long it took; she was saving herself for him.

Chapter 15

Before the baby was a year old, Jake told Dorn and Raistlin it was time to hike through the Dark Forest. Their eyes lit up like they were kids again. It was something they had longed to do for over a decade.

Years before, when they were young enough to camp on their own and when the river was low and slow, they floated on a raft to the other side and then hiked to the edge of the trees and out into the open fields. In the distance, the Dark Forest stood with its tall trees, the tallest in all of Evergreen. Above the trees, an eternal storm spewed lightning, and constant rumbles could be heard even though they were half a day's hike from the forest. The boys would watch in awe, knowing someday the time would come.

They gathered their things and donned leather backpacks. Nana and Tessa made them especially for the trek. The shoulder straps were padded with wool, which was more forgiving on the shoulders when they carried a heavy load.

The trek through the forest lived up to all the folklore they had heard about as children. They hiked with torches in their hands due to the darkness of the forest. The dark clouds overhead blocked out most of the sunlight, and the canopy at the tops of the trees fought for whatever light they could muster. The storm whipped the tops of the trees back and forth, but with constant moisture on the trees, the branches flew back and forth like whips, never losing a branch or a leaf.

When the trio reached the heart of the forest, the climate was drastically different. The clouds were thinner, and it was bitter cold. The trees were fragile with ice, and the occasional branch would drop to the hard ground as they hiked.

There was enough sunlight through the thin clouds and the lack of a canopy to make their way without torches, but they still carried them for extra warmth.

Hours later, they spotted a polar bear through the trees. Its size was impressive.

Jake stooped down when he saw the bear and held his torch down. "Lower your flames," he said.

Raistlin and Dorn dropped to their knees and held their flames behind their backs. Jake looked around, then pointed to the right.

"This way," he said. He scurried off, keeping a low profile and holding the torch to the ground.

"Hurry," he whispered to the others.

They raced toward a vast dark shadow that seemed ominous and towered before them. It was a rock wall that went beyond the height of the trees. At its base, they found a cave. They waited until they thought the polar bear was no longer a threat, then they tossed their torches onto the floor and tossed on a few more branches that were left in the cave.

"Who left the firewood here?" Raistlin asked.

Jake looked at him. The fire reflected in his eyes. "I did," he said. "This spot doesn't move, but the rest of the forest will."

"What do you mean?" Raistlin asked.

"Let's get some rest, you'll see," Jake said.

Once the fire was blazing and they were warm, they all curled up on the cave floor and snoozed with their heads resting on their backpacks.

#

The cold woke them. Raistlin was the first to rise and saw coals glowing where the fire was when they fell asleep. He grabbed more branches, and soon, flames were dancing before them. Once the light reached beyond the mouth of the cave, Raistlin leaned forward to try to get a better look.

"Things did move, didn't they?" he asked.

Jake looked out and nodded, "It is always moving, but it's so slow you can hardly see it."

"Why is it always moving?" Dorn asked.

"To throw off the traveler." Jake found three decent sticks to make torches and put the knotty ends into the fire. "A path or a trail will never stay in the Dark Forest. Many get lost in here and never make it out."

"And they die?" Raistlin asked.

Jake nodded. "Some of the caves in this rock wall have skeletons in them."

Raistlin and Dorn gave each other a weary look.

"Why didn't we fly around the forest on the dragons like you always do?" Raistlin asked.

"Because you two are young men now. You have to experience the Dark Forest; this won't be your last time here." Jake grabbed one of the torches and stood. "Grab your torches."

The other two each grabbed a torch and stood. Jake looked each of them in the eyes one at a time.

"Stay strong," he said. "Once fatigue sets in, this place will mess with your mind. Stick together. We have a long way to go."

Jake turned and walked out of the cave, gripping the torch and holding it to his side.

Jake was typically relaxed and jovial in his everyday life. He did what needed to be done with a smile, and when the chores and jobs were finished, he relaxed with his family and longed to see everyone else smile. Since they had approached the Dark Forest and stood and stared at it in the distance, Jake's demeanor was not what it usually was. He didn't smile. His words were quick and sharp, and his eyes darted to the sides often. His movements were smooth and calculated. There was no time for chit-chat. The only time Dorn and Raistlin had seen Jake so serious was the day Dorn's father was murdered.

The trek through the forest did take a toll on them. They grew tired often, and none could recall how long they had been in the forest. They spoke of it briefly over a fire in one of the caves. Raistlin thought it had been five days. Dorn thought they were on their third day. Jake said it had probably been two days since they entered the forest. They slept in small increments and continued to hike when they woke. Once the food in their packs was exhausted, Dorn tied his dagger to a long, straight branch. He tied it with vines that he cut from the trees.

Throughout the trek through the forest, they spotted Hokies. Dorn and Raistlin had only heard stories about them because they were not seen anywhere else in Evergreen; it was a creature that only lived in the Dark Forest. Once they realized they were out of food, hunting was the only option because it was too cold for vegetation to grow.

Dorn sat in the crotch of a tree with his makeshift spear in hand. Raistlin walked several dozen yards away in a circle, trying to stir up whatever small animals he could. Soon, a Hokie walked under Dorn, and he speared it on the first try.

They cooked a Hokie on a stick and could barely finish eating the small animal between the three of them. Although the taste was gamey and bland, the protein packed a punch. Soon, they were trekking again. The dark skies above them continued to swirl. Constant flashes of lightning and rumbles of thunder became the norm.

Aside from the horrible weather, from nasty storms to bitter cold and then back to bad storms, the remainder of their trek was uneventful.

When they walked out of the Dark Forest, grass plains lay before them. The three men took a deep breath of clean air and walked away from the tall trees. The breeze was refreshing, and the sunlight felt great on them after several days of darkness and cold.

Dorn looked over his shoulder and glanced at the sky behind him. It swirled like a witch's brew, and lightning stretched to the edge of the dark clouds.

As they walked through the grass field, Jake put his arms around each of them and smiled for the first time in days. Jake was slightly shorter than the other two, and his short hair showed the slightest gray traces. Raistlin's shoulder length brown hair was trapped under Jake's arm. When Raistlin smiled, he showed handsome white teeth and a wide mouth.

Dorn's hair was black, and he always kept it short, and his dark eyes were both inviting and intimidating.

In the other world, there were cameras, devices that could catch moments in time. If someone had had a camera as the trio walked away from the tall trees and the dark skies above, they would have been able to take a photo of the ages of a trio that was happy as ever with the sunlight beating down on them, but the skies and trees in the darkness behind them. It could have been a photo for a movie poster or an album cover. It would have been grand. It would have been one of the greatest candid photos of all time.

#

Although they were a half day hike past the Dark Forest, they could still see the storm's anger in the distance when they camped that evening. They cooked fish Dorn had caught from the nearby river and ate blackberries they had picked near the bank. They rested their heads on their packs with stars overhead, and rumbles of thunder in the distance lulled them to sleep.

The next morning, they ate more blackberries and brewed rose hip tea in a small pan that had rattled against the back of Jake's backpack for their entire hike. They drank the tea from small tin cups that also hung from his pack during the trek.

Soon, they were hiking along the river again. By midday, they walked into a clearing. In the distance was a small cabin. To the left were two small barns and a mountain range behind them.

Dorn and Raistlin had heard about the cabin up north, and even though it was smaller than they had imagined, they were still in awe of visiting a place that had been in their thoughts since they were young boys.

Randall walked out the door onto the porch as they approached the cabin. He hunched over his cane and smiled at the group.

"Welcome to the cabin up north," he said. "How was the Dark Forest?"

"Pretty uneventful," Jake said.

"Didn't see the Yeti?" Randall asked.

Jake shook his head.

"What's a Yeti?" Raistlin asked.

"It's a big, hairy, white beast," Randall held his arms up as if describing how tall the beast was. His cane hung from his right hand. "Must be about nine feet tall. He only lives in the Dark Forest."

Raistlin and Dorn shared a glance and a grin with each other.

"I don't think the boys believe me, Jake," Randall said.

"Maybe they will see him on the hike back to the homestead," Jake said and grinned at Randall.

#

Over a campfire that night, Jake told Raistlin and Dorn they would head home when it was time.

"I have to get your grandfather back to the homestead," Jake said. "He isn't getting around as well as he used to, and he can't handle the chores here. I will often go between here and the homestead. The dragons need training, and we are also trying to start a homestead here."

#

For five days, they did as much as they could. They built chicken coops and mended the fence extending from the barn's corner. The fence was only there for cosmetic purposes; otherwise, it served no purpose in what was pretty much no man's land. Randall and Jake thought it would look nice if a split rail fence came off the barn.

With one of the dragons pulling the plow, they cultivated the garden. They planted corn, onions, peas, carrots, tomatoes, green beans, and celery. They tidied up the barn and built a hanging contraption for slaughtering big game. They killed a ram, dressed it, and readied the hide for tanning. They cut the horns from the skull, which Randall would later use to make a bugle type instrument. They chopped and stacked enough wood to last for months. The cold months of Evergreen demanded some wood to keep homes warm, but most of the wood was used for cooking, whether in a kitchen wood stove, or on a campfire.

Chapter 16

Raistlin and Dorn stood in the grass at the base of the stairs that led to the porch. Randall sat in a wooden patio chair, and Jake leaned against the rail. The evening before, Raistlin and Dorn learned they would be hiking through the Dark Forest alone. Jake and Randall were to fly back soon on the dragons. So, with both excitement and trepidation, they gathered their things that morning and prepared for the journey home.

As they bid their goodbyes and were on their way, Jake hollered to them, "Watch out for that Yeti!"

Raistlin and Dorn looked at each other and laughed.

#

It turned out the warning was correct, and the folklore was authentic: a Yeti did live in the Dark Forest.

On the north side of the forest, the weather is always colder, and the storms either consist of ice or snow. Much of the area is glazed over in ice, and the canopy above is brittle and lacks leaves, which causes the forest floor to give off a soft glow from the light that seeps through the dark clouds. It is much easier to see the trees and wildlife in this part of the forest than any other.

They lit new torches while they waited under a rock outcropping. Once the storm lulled, they made their way into the forest again. After several minutes, Dorn held out his hand, and both men stopped walking.

"Don't move," Dorn whispered.

Raistlin glanced at Dorn and then followed his line of sight. Under a tree, a furry, white hand seemed to glow in the torch's light. The hand was huge, almost as big as either of their heads. The rest of the creature was hidden under the shadows of the tree. The fingers on the hand moved, and then the creature's arm came into view as it slowly moved toward them.

The men remained frozen, knowing they were no match for the beast, although Dorn slid his hand onto the pommel of his sword. He'd only been carrying the sword since moving back into his house. It was a sense of protection for him. Daily, he thought of the day his father was murdered, the abrupt finality of the event. He never knew when the same situation might arise for him, and he did not want to share the same fate as his father.

As the beast moved closer to them, more of its body became visible. After another small step, the entire creature was in their view. The beast was huge, nearly nine feet tall, as Randall had described. The white fur on the arms, legs, and torso was much thicker than on the hands and feet. Its face resembled that of an ape but with white fur covering it. Its eyes were blue and glued on the two men standing before it.

The men held their breath as the Yeti looked them over. Once satisfied, the Yeti snorted and looked off into the darkness of the forest. Then it began to walk away. A slight breeze crept by and blew the hair on its back for a moment. Raistlin held his torch higher to better look at the beast as it began to disappear.

"Great Fathers, I thought our gooses were cooked," Raistlin whispered.

"Me too," Dorn said. The torchlight reflected in his eyes as he watched the Yeti disappear into the darkness.

#

49

Soon, they were back at the homestead. Jake and Randall had flown in days before. After a few more days, Jake and Nana flew out on two of the dragons to start their life at the cabin north of the Dark Forest.

Chapter 17

In the middle of the cold season, Randall passed during a clear night when the Harvest Moon was full. A dove had been sent to the cabin days earlier, warning Jake and Nana that Randall's days were dwindling.

Dorn and Raistlin rode together on the seat of the wagon as America pulled them to the mill. They entered the mill long before the sun appeared over the horizon, and the birds in the trees began singing their morning songs.

Hours later, the two men were loading a wooden casket onto the wagon.

The following day, in typical ritual for most of those from Ironwood, Randall Barrow was buried at the base of Rickenback Mountain.

Chapter 18

As Cambria grew older, she experimented more and more with roots, concoctions, and remedies. When something ailed someone, she found a cure through her instinctive knowledge and the information she absorbed from the books she read.

Her talents became known in town, and there were times when the local doctor in Ironwood would call on her to help him with a remedy.

Raistlin and Tessa were proud of Cambria and her abilities. They were happy she could help others with ailments and sicknesses, but the word spread.

Since the fight on the bridge between Dorn Hale and Lance Erickson years earlier, the townspeople on each side of the river kept to their own business. But some ventured to the other side with the sole responsibility of bringing back news of anything pertinent to Ironwood. Soon, reports were coming back that Ivan Erickson had taken ill and was on his deathbed at the top of Erikson's Castle. With the popularity of Cambria's abilities, the word worked its way across the river. Rumors swirled that Lance Erikson wanted to find out more information about Cambria.

#

When the rumor reached the Barrow Homestead, Raistlin was nonchalant about it. He laughed it off. He even considered it an opportunity to fix the severed ties between the two towns. He and Dorn didn't see eye to eye on the subject.

"The guy is a lunatic," Dorn pointed at Raistlin. They sat in wooden chairs by a campfire at their usual fire pit halfway between Raistlin's and Dorn's houses. "He will do anything to get what he wants."

"What are you saying?" Raistlin asked.

"You need to protect Cambria," Dorn said as he looked into the fire.

"From what?" Raistlin asked.

Dorn raised his eyes from the fire and looked at Raistlin, "Don't be naive, Raistlin."

Raistlin leaned back in his chair and held his hands out for a moment, signaling that he was lost in the conversation.

"He will kidnap your daughter," Dorn said with a stern look.

Raistlin's eyes widened, "What?"

"I know it's a worst case scenario," Dorn said. "But don't rule it out."

Raistlin lowered his head and closed his eyes for a moment. When he looked up, he said, "So, what do I do?"

Dorn looked back into the fire and quietly said, "Send her up north, and don't tell a soul."

Raistlin leaned back in his chair, looked to the stars, and thought about Dorn's suggestion.

#

The rumor that came back to Greystone was that the girl with the special powers had disappeared. Lance was desperate to find a way to make his father healthy again. He sent spies across the river to learn more about the girl's whereabouts.

Lance never thought it was worth it to venture into the Dark Forest, and he never thought there would be anything worthwhile on the other side. He had no idea Cambria was on the north side of the forest.

When he knew she was nowhere to be found, Lance launched a mission to track her down. His idea of how to find her was something nobody in Evergreen could have ever imagined.

Lance knew that the Barrow family had taken several trips to the other world, the world many people lived in before they came to Evergreen. Lance and his father had also taken trips to that world. The path to that world was through the In Between, labeled for precisely what it was: a path between two worlds. Many in Evergreen knew their homeland was unique and that the other world was tainted with war and evil.

The path was simple: a mysterious door on a wall or a forest floor. The door was small, as was the tunnel to the other world, which was usually a straight shot through the tunnel to the other door.

When Lance was not in Evergreen, he had strong magical powers. In the other world, he could shapeshift, and any others working with him could shapeshift as well.

He became convinced that Cambria Barrow was nowhere to be found in Evergreen. The only other option was that she was in the other world, which was much too big of a place to go looking for a twelve year old girl.

In his mind, Lance had his Gods to whom he prayed. One day, as he sat in the tunnel of the In Between, he prayed to have workers there with him.

When he opened his eyes, four people were before him: two males and two females. They wore white hardhats and denim overalls with white shirts underneath. One of the females had a blonde ponytail draped out of her hard hat; the other had a red ponytail.

"Whatcha need now, boss," the tall one said.

Lance's troubled look slowly turned to a grin.

The workers worked day and night without taking breaks or sleeping. Days turned into weeks as Lance supervised the work and kept putting in his requests. He was overseeing the transformation of the In Between. One straight tunnel soon became a series of intertwined tunnels and eventually became a labyrinth. At the end of every tunnel was an archway. Lance watched as the construction workers built wooden arched forms to hold the stone and mortar until the mortar cured. Then, the wooden forms were removed, and the stone arches stood. Lance was amazed at the craftsmanship shown by the workers. Another thing he noticed was that they never grew tired, and their clothes never dirtied. He was also surprised at the workers' cohesiveness; people in the other world would say they worked like a well-oiled machine.

At the end of every arched tunnel was a large area. In one area, there was a pond with banks covered with flat rocks. The rocks would be tossed onto the water one by one with a sidearm throw. The thrower hoped for as many skips across the water as possible, a game that could keep kids busy for hours. Another tunnel may lead to a baseball diamond, or a real-life Super Mario Bros game, both were popular things in the other world.

Then Lance had doors built and installed. They were arched walnut doors with aged brass hardware. The doors were shorter than most, which Lance thought may attract a child. They were placed not only all over the In Between but also in the other world.

Lance's magic in the In Between was stronger than anyone had imagined. His doors, which were placed in the other world, had no time frame. In other words, any door in the other world that led to the In Between could be from any year, month, or day in other world time. Someone from the Napoleonic Era could enter the In Between at the same time as someone from Cold War Era Soviet Union. If those two stood face to face in the In Between, they would have a problem communicating with the language barrier, but in one of their worlds, the other person was centuries dead.

During one of his meditations, Lance heard his Gods tell him he was flirting with disaster by making these portals to different times. If anyone entered the In Between and left through another door, that person would be traveling time. This was something the Gods said could lead to devastating consequences.

Lance scoffed at the idea and put their warnings out of his head.

#

He spent years searching for Cambria. He visited the In Between several times a week. He thought if she were in the other world she might stumble upon the door and venture to the In Between. Occasionally, a child would get lost in the In Between's labyrinth. Lance's helpers would inform him of this, and he would come to the rescue.

His idea of a rescue was to charm the child and eventually take the child back to Greystone. It was easy to charm the children. Although Lance was self-centered, arrogant, and demeaning, he could pour on the charm. He had a nice smile, and once the children warmed up to him, they admired his tattooed arms and piercings.

Lance fostered these children and realized he could expand his power by training them. Then, he started to take children from Greystone. He planned to build onto the castle and use the children as servants, cooks, and an army. He would expand on the castle after his father was gone.

#

Once Jake and Nana were settled at the cabin, Cambria was sent north to stay with them. Raistlin and Dorn took her through the Dark Forest. The only other option was to fly there on a dragon. They didn't like that idea in case someone was watching and saw dragons flying a long distance away from the homestead.

"What did The Great Fathers say about this?" Jake asked once Raistlin explained what was happening and why he wanted Cambria to stay at the cabin.

Raistlin shook his head and said, "I haven't mentioned it. I'm sure they know by now."

"They know everything," Jake said.

Over the next several years, close attention was paid to the Greystone side of the river. Dorn often went on spy missions with Fitz and Milo. Fitz was a huge asset to the Barrow Homestead. He was knowledgeable and good at problem solving. He kept to himself, but when he was asked, he always delivered. He was also a good fighter, handy with the sword, but not quite as good as Raistlin, Dorn, or Lance Erikson.

Not in a million years would Dorn Hale have thought he would kill Fitz one day.

Milo was dedicated as well. He wasn't sharp like Fitz, but he was committed. Dorn and Raistlin didn't lean on Milo as much as they did with Fitz. Milo had a problem with the booze and would get looselipped at the tavern. He was fine on their excursions, like hunts and spy missions. The only booze available on those trips was what each of them brought in their flasks. It was a controlled environment. But it was a different story when Milo was in the bar with a pocket full of coins.

The others that were dedicated to the Barrow family were Hawley and Zed. Fitz, Mylo, Hawley, and Zed all worked at the lumber mill that Raistlin and Dorn owned. They also dedicated their spare time to the homestead and the family. Zed was usually at his own homestead. He spent much of his time breeding hunting dogs. When it was time to hunt, Zed always led the way with two or three of the best dogs in Evergreen.

Hawley was a good friend. He helped with whatever needed to be done. He always wore a cowboy hat and looked older than his years. He never had any business carrying a sword, but when it came time to use his fists, his opponent usually ended up eating humble pie.

The last true dedication to the homestead was a man named Abraham Polk. He was the blacksmith in town who had grown to be great friends of Dorn, Raistlin, and Sally. The first meeting was a peculiar one. Dorn had been replacing a broken window in the saloon for Sally. He was trimming it when he glanced out the window; a nail was between his lips.

Abraham stood in the middle of the street, looking lost. He wore coveralls with no shirt underneath. His black boots were unlaced. Moments later, Dorn was at his side asking questions.

Abraham was invited into the saloon and sat with Dorn and Sally. Abraham had an ale while Dorn and Sally sipped on whiskey. They learned that Abraham had been doing blacksmith work when he felt a sudden pain in his chest.

"Next thing I know," Abraham said. "I'm standin' in the middle of your town, wondering what in Heavens to Betsy just happened."

"You're a blacksmith?" Dorn asked.

"Yessuh," Abraham said.

Dorn glanced at Sally, and they both smiled.

Abraham moved into Sally's vacant apartment and took over the blacksmith's shop. Many of his meals were at the saloon, allowing him to get to know the townspeople. He loved drinking a beer or two, but nothing beyond that. Occasionally, he was tasked with kicking someone out or breaking up a fight. He often walked to the Barrow Homestead from town to have a few of "Mistah Raistlin's" homebrewed ales. After sitting by the fire and a few ales, Abraham would always walk back to town regardless of the complaints of him not taking one of the horses.

As time passed, Abraham was as close to the homestead as anyone else.

Not long after Cambria was shipped up north, Tessa became pregnant. Nana and Cambria flew down on a dragon once the weeks of the pregnancy wound down. On a rainy night, Anastasia was born. Cambria was the first to hold her, and days later, Cambria headed north, so the two sisters didn't see each other for several years.

#

Dorn always took it upon himself to set up patrols on either side of the river, and Dorn, Fitz, and Mylo were snooping around the woods south of Greystone when Billy Blaine fell from the sky.

This was Billy's first trip to Evergreen from the sky. He would later do it again but in a much grander fashion with a bear head as a cap.

Fitz stepped forward when Lance struck the boy after a short argument. They drew their swords and faced off, and after a few swipes of their swords, Fitz was struck on the shoulder and went to the ground. Dorn stepped into the moonlight and drew his sword. That is when Lance disappeared with a swoop of his long coat.

Fitz thought everything had gone well. He was just as surprised as Dorn and Mylo that Lance had fallen from the sky with a young boy, but his willingness to fight Lance took away any doubt of his loyalty to Dorn and Raistlin.

His approach to fighting Lance was a farce. He and Lance knew it and knew that Lance could have hurt him much more than he did.

For over a year, Fitz communicated with some of Lance's men. One of them was Boris Wagner, the blonde swordfighter. Boris was the most cautious of Lance's men; he rarely trusted anyone. He took his time infiltrating Raistlin's circle in search of slumber sand.

It took a dragon to make slumber sand, and the Barrow family were the only ones in Evergreen that owned dragons. Lance had heard of the benefits of slumber sand and wanted some for himself. He wanted it to give to his father, who was up at the top of the castle, dying a long and agonizing death. The slumber sand would relieve his symptoms for a time.

Chapter 19

A dragon's fire is unique, more unique than any other flame in the universe. Humankind has devised ingenious ways to utilize fire, particularly in warfare. From flaming arrows to napalm and nuclear weapons, fire is the ultimate weapon. It is the same for a dragon; a dragon's fire can catch nearly anything on fire, and that fire can spread quickly.

When she was nine years old, just a few years before she was shipped north, Cambria began to study dragon's fire out of curiosity. With Dorn's help, she had Celeste breathe fire on many different things; then, she would dissect the things that had been scorched. Things like tree branches, apples, iron, various species of wood, or dead animal parts. Soon, she began concocting powdered mixtures and had Celeste scorch her recipes. Time after time, nothing came out of the experiments except a small pile of charred ingredients.

One morning, she woke from a dream with excitement. The dream had given her an idea. She spent the morning finding different roots and seeds. She shaved the roots, crushed the seeds, and pulverized both into a powder. They backed away as Celeste shot a short flame onto the small pile. The pile of powder melted into a blob, similar to a blob of glass. Once the blob cooled, Cambria placed it on a stone bench and began to crush it with a wooden mallet. She pounded up and down, sometimes with both hands, as the blob turned into a pile of powder that was almost clear. When she was satisfied, she gathered it all and poured it into a small leather pouch, then hung the pouch around her neck.

"Want to see if it works?" She looked at Dorn as she headed for the door of the barn.

Dorn nodded and followed her out.

She headed for the chicken coop. The chickens gathered at the short water trough outside their nesting quarters. They all perked their heads as she approached, hoping for a handout. Cambria reached into her pocket and pulled out some crushed corn crumbles. She sprinkled a few on the ground. The chickens bumped into each other as they scrambled for the yellow prizes. She lured one of the hens toward her and held the feed in her hand as she squatted. The chicken began pecking out of her hand; Cambria pulled a pinch of her new concoction out of the leather pouch with her other hand. She wiped the clear powder onto the beak near its nostrils as the hen ate out of her hand. The chicken stumbled for a moment, then fell onto its side and lay motionless.

Dorn quickly stepped forward. Cambria held out her hand, "It's okay." Cambria picked up the chicken and held it close to her. She looked up at Dorn and said, "She is still breathing."

"How did you do that?" Dorn asked.

Cambria shrugged her shoulders and smiled. "Let's take her to the barn," she said.

Once they were back at the barn, Cambria set the chicken on the bench; it continued to lay in a motionless slumber.

"Keep an eye on her," Dorn said. "I have to run to town."

#

When the barn door opened again, both Dorn and Raistlin walked through. Cambria looked up from her seat on the bench and smiled at them. The hen that had been asleep when Dorn left earlier in the afternoon was on the floor pecking away at corn that had been scattered.

Dorn turned to Raistlin, "The hen was sleeping when I left."

Raistlin walked to where Cambria sat. She had a piece of parchment on the table with some figures on it. "What are you working on?" he asked.

"I am trying to figure out the ratio of how much I gave her to how long she slept compared to how much she weighs."

"How did you make her fall asleep," Raistlin asked.

Cambria held the leather pouch out to him. Raistlin took it, loosened the rawhide strap that tied it closed, and dipped his finger into the pouch. He pulled it out and rubbed his finger and thumb together as the tiny crystals floated to the ground.

"I think we should call it slumber sand," Cambria said, smiling.

Chapter 20

Although tensions between Ironwood and Greystone were always high, a little negotiation between Lance and Raistlin may have gone a long way. Had Lance stated his case to Raistlin, that he wanted slumber sand to make his ailing father more comfortable, Raistlin would have worked up a trade or even given him some of the slumber sand in his cache. But Lance would not approach him. Part of it was pride, and part of it was lunacy.

So, Lance demanded Boris to find a way to get slumber sand. Boris picked Fitz to try to work on. The other obvious choice was a short, bald man named Mylo, who worked with the goats. He looked like he was too easy of a target, and he often got long winded at the saloon, which could become a problem if he began speaking about something he wasn't supposed to discuss. Boris ultimately decided Fitz was the one to convince him to help him. The only problem, Boris learned, was that only four people had access to the slumber sand. One was Cambria, but she hadn't been seen publicly in nearly a decade. The others were Raistlin, Dorn, and Mylo. Mylo had access to the slumber sand because he slaughtered the goats. The goats were a huge asset to the homestead, dead or alive. To kill the goats as humanely as possible, they were put to sleep with slumber sand before their necks were sliced to drain their life's blood.

"Look," Fitz had said to Mylo. "I have some land I could give you. I need that slumber sand."

"What for?" Mylo said.

"My wife, for starters," Fitz said, looking at Mylo with his fierce eyes. "You know she has been sick, Mylo."

Mylo's shoulders slumped, and he soon agreed to get Fitz some medicine. Unfortunately, skipping the goat's dose was the only way to get the medicine. Dorn and Raistlin kept a close eye on the medicine inventory. When Mylo took some to put down a goat, it was recorded. To keep the inventory correct, he had to kill some goats without the medicine and pass it off to Fitz.

Mylo had dreamed of having his land. Raising his animals for milk, meat, and other things. The tradeoff was good enough in his eyes. He could hide the slumber sand and kill the goats with no meds as long as nobody was in the barn with him. He had no trouble putting animals down; he had done it since he was young while working on a farm with his father. It was all for a good cause. And when he was young, there was no slumber sand. An animal didn't feel a ton of pain when a tiny slit was cut in their neck to drain blood from the jugular.

One morning, after a drunken night at the saloon, Fitz came to Mylo's cabin and woke him. Fitz was furious about what he had heard. Mylo had talked a little too much while drunk and possibly gave away some secrets between him and Fitz.

Fitz hid his anger under his charm and told Mylo he was taking him to stake out his new land. Mylo was immediately excited, regardless of his hungover state.

Fitz had Mylo don a backpack. "You'll only need things for a few days," Fitz told him. Mylo didn't notice that Fitz had packed more in his backpack.

They hiked for a day, then camped under the night sky that seemed to go forever over the vast plains of Evergreen. Stars lit the sky from one horizon to the other. The Dragon Moon was the brightest of the three, giving off its white light. The Prophet's Moon was only a partial moon that evening; the furthest extent of its red hue mixed with the purple color of the Traveler's Moon, creating a colorful night sky. The night was beautiful, and they decided not to light a fire. They munched on salted goat meat, and Fitz drew a metal flask from his pack and passed it to Mylo.

"Aye," Mylo said and took the flask. He seemed exhausted from the long hike.

"We have another long hike tomorrow, my friend," Fitz said. They passed the flask back and forth, then Fitz waved it off and let Mylo enjoy it for himself. "Sip away. You look exhausted."

Just as Fitz wanted, it wasn't long before Mylo was chatting away.

"Where is my new land, Fitzy?" Mylo asked and took another swig from the flask.

"It will be a few days yet."

"Why so far? This seems much farther away than I thought." Mylo said.

"So far from what?"

"Everything. The Barrow Homestead. Ironwood."

"You won't need any of that," Fitz said. "You will have some of the best farmland in all of Evergreen. You can bring some help with you and build your homestead."

"How will I pay anyone to help me?"

"Mylo, you've done a great thing for me. I have enough slumber sand to keep my wife comfortable through her sickness. Great Fathers, Mylo, I have enough slumber sand to kill a dragon." Fitz tilted his head back and laughed.

Mylo busted up in laughter, but after a few moments, Fitz stopped laughing and looked off into the darkness with a cold stare while Mylo continued to laugh.

After Mylo finished laughing, Fitz asked, "Mylo, how many people have you told about our little secret?"

"Aye, secret," Mylo tilted his head back. It was evident that the whiskey was bearing down on him with full force. "Hmm, only a few."

"Who?" Fitz asked.

"Hmm," Mylo said, then he looked at Fitz. "Does it matter?"

Fitz gave him a friendly smile and said, "Ah, you are right. If they are your friends, then we can trust them."

"Aye," Mylo said and leaned back against his pack. In moments, he was snoring.

Fitz leaned his head back on his pack and looked up at the stars, knowing that at that very moment, Boris and Scud were killing one of Raistlin's dragons.

#

The next morning, they continued their hike to the river. They untied a raft from a tree and pushed it out into the water. Soon, they were on the other side of the river. They left the raft behind and continued to hike. Once they were in a clearing again, they could see the eternal storm twisting and turning over The Dark Forest. Every few seconds, lightning danced across the sky.

"Where's my land, Fitz?" Mylo asked. "Why are we approaching The Dark Forest?"

Fitz walked in silence for a few moments, then said, "We have some herbs and seeds we can get at the edge of the forest; then we can find your land and stake it out."

"Aye," Mylo said.

They walked closer and closer to the forest. The air cooled as they approached the massive trees. Thunder constantly rumbled.

Large rocks littered the edge of the forest. Some of them were the size of watermelons, some of them the size of a small cabin. They weaseled their way through the rocks, and instead of going into the woods, Fitz led the way to walk the edge of the forest, weaving through the rocks as they went.

"Where are the herbs?" Mylo asked.

"Right about here," Fitz stopped and looked around. The dark sky slowly swirled over their heads. "I have something to take care of."

"Aye, what would that be?"

"I am going to trek through The Dark Forest and go to Raistlin's cabin up north."

"They've given you permission to go there?" Mylo asked.

"No, stupid. I am going by my own will."

"Through The Dark Forest?"

"Yes."

Mylo looked up at the tops of the trees. "I've never done that."

"And you're not going to. You are staying here," he took half a step toward Mylo. "I will capture Cambria and take her to Erikson's Castle, and she will cure Ivan Erikson."

"Ye are in dealings with Lance?"

Fitz nodded.

"How could you?" Mylo's voice began to quiver.

"How could I? How could you?" Fitz said.

"Me?"

"Remember all the slumber sand I had, do you see now?"

"Aye, that's why we are here."

"You are correct," Fitz said. "That sand wasn't for my wife. I accumulated enough to kill a dragon."

Mylo turned his head slightly to the side and glared at Fitz.

"One of Raislin's dragons is dead right now," Fitz said.

"No," Mylo's eyes glassed.

"Yes," Fitz said. "Because of you. You are a traitor now."

"You never told me," Mylo was on the verge of crying. "I didn't know."

"You'll be fine," Fitz said. "You can sleep here. I'll wake you when I get back."

"What?" Mylo asked. His anxiety caused him to speak in the accent of his land.

Fitz threw a handful of slumber sand into Mylo's face. Mylo fell to the ground, bumping his head on a rock. He was out like a light.

Fitz turned Mylo over so he was face down. He pulled his dagger from its sheath. He put his hand on Mylo's forehead and pulled his head up. Then he pressed his dagger to Mylo's neck. He pressed harder, and the sharp edge pushed through the skin and severed the jugular. Blood squirted from his neck a few times, then the flow slowed, and a pool of red began to seep between the pebbles on the ground. Fitz looked at Mylo for a time as his life drained away. His eyes never wavered, and they were as cold as ice. He took a deep breath, looked at his surroundings, and sheathed his dagger. Then he grabbed his pack, turned, and walked into The Dark Forest.

Chapter 21

Dorn did his best to comfort Billy and make him feel like a part of the family, both with himself and the Barrow family. Billy spent much of his time with Anastasia, and Dorn noticed that he seemed less homesick when he was with her.

Dorn assisted Tessa, Raistlin's wife, with the duties around the homestead while Raistlin was away trying to pluck the Collins brothers from the real world. However, Tessa could have taken care of the homestead duties herself.

When Raistlin returned with a lanky young lad and his older brother on the Day of the Feast, the world shifted a little for Dorn. Dorn felt as though he already knew the lanky lad since he had spent weeks listening to Billy carry on about him but knew nothing of the older brother except that he had taken advice that had been given to him years before from a young man from Corktown. The older brother had taken information from the future and changed the outcome, creating a paradox. This turned Lance's life and the In Between upside down.

Not only had Jared single-handedly and unknowingly destroyed the In Between for a short time, but he had also saved many of his comrades from an attack that would have killed several of them, including himself. He had cheated death, and he was a war hero. Dorn felt that this deserved the ultimate honor. Jared's personality and seriousness of situations lived up to the honor that Dorn gave. It sparked a wonderful friendship that would impact both men for the remainder of their lives.

#

Several hours after Raistlin, Jared, Josh, and Billy walked away on their trek to the cabin up north, the sound of the horse's trot on the stone road caught Dorn's attention. Zed came streaking up the road on his horse. Two of his bird dogs, one a pointer, the other a spaniel, trailed him and his horse.

Zed pulled his horse to a stop, and before Dorn could say anything, Zed said, "Mylo is dead."

Dorn thought he was dreaming for a moment, then gave Zed a stern look and said, "What?"

"I found Mylo at the edge of The Dark Forest. He was murdered," Zed said.

Dorn was lost for words.

"Have you seen Fitz since Celeste was," Zed trailed off.

Dorn shook his head.

"I saw footsteps," Zed took a deep breath. "Footsteps not far from Mylo's body. They led into The Dark Forest."

"We need to go there," Dorn said.

"We'll have to go around and up to the shallow crossing on the Black," Zed said. "We'll have to go on horseback."

Dorn nodded, "I'll pack my bag and get Cherokee. I'll meet you at the bridge."

Zed nodded, spun his horse around, and nudged its sides with his boot heels. The horse trotted down the road, and the dogs followed. A fog of dust floated in the air after they rounded the bend.

#

When Dorn met him at the bridge, Zed had a sleeping roll and a small pack tied down behind his saddle. They took the bridge out of Ironwood, crossed the river, hugged the riverbank, and headed north. They rode quickly and low in the saddle to avoid anyone seeing them. The dogs followed but had been ordered by Zed before they traversed the bridge to remain quiet. They rode for miles, never allowing the horses to go slower than a trot. They rode past the confluence of the Black and the Snake Rivers and continued north. They were traveling upriver, so the banks grew closer together, and rocks began to poke through the water more and more.

When the water was shallow enough to cross, they let the horses stop and drink from the river. The dogs also waded and lapped up the clean river water. Once on the other side, Dorn and Zed slipped down from their saddles and let the horses graze for a while. The dogs stretched out on the grass, panting.

Dorn and Zed stood side by side, reins in their hands while their horses grazed behind them, and looked at the swirl of dark clouds and the lightning bolts that jetted across the sky above the Dark Forest. Soon, they were on their horses and headed toward the mayhem.

Zed's dogs led them to the spot in the large rocks to Mylo's body. Zed looked at Dorn and nodded.

Dorn climbed down from Cherokee, handed the leather reins to Zed, and then walked to the body. He stood for a time with his head bowed and returned to Zed.

"I have to track those footsteps," Dorn said. "I think Raistlin may get ambushed. I have to stay ahead of it."

"Do you want me to go with you?" Zed asked.

"No," Dorn looked at him. "Take Cherokee with you. I need you to watch over the homestead."

Zed nodded.

Dorn pointed to the coiled rope hanging from Zed's saddle, "Can I take your rope?"

"Of course," Zed said, untying the rope from his saddle. Then he cut a small section of the rope with his knife and handed the rest to Dorn."Be safe."

"I will," Dorn said and held out his hand for a handshake. Zed took his hand, and Dorn pulled him in for a quick hug. Then he turned without looking back, tossed his pack over his shoulder, and followed the footprints into the Dark Forest.

Zed led the horses a few hundred yards away from the edge of the forest and tied them to trees where they could graze. He rounded up some dry branches and made a fire that lasted long enough for him to brew a cup of tea. He tossed each dog a piece of salted goat meat and then tugged on one himself as he sipped the hot tea.

Once he finished with the tea, he crawled into his sleeping bag and used his pack for a pillow. The Spaniel curled up against the back of his legs and was asleep long before Zed. The Pointer lay on the edge of the glow of the fire. Her nose was between her front paws, constantly sniffing the air, and her eyes glanced at the sky with every lightning bolt that danced over her head.

The following morning, Zed draped Mylo's body over Cherokee. He tied him to the saddle with the portion of rope he kept for himself the evening before. Then, they trotted toward the Black River.

Chapter 22

Fitz had meddled in The Dark Forest once in the past. He had hiked it, hoping to see what was on the other side. He went alone and learned how things constantly changed and that the storm overhead was constant and sometimes relentless.

After killing Mylo, he trekked through the forest again and slept when he could. His focus and mature sense of direction got him through with no issues.

After being out of the Dark Forest for a second day, Fitz camped in a heavy wood with rough terrain. He found a spot of tall grass to spread his sleeping bag under a tree. He did not have a fire. He was smart enough to know that someone from the homestead had figured out what was happening, and they could be coming after him. He didn't want to give himself up with the smell of smoke that could drift for miles. He leaned against the tree and sipped from his flask. Dusk grew to dark, and soon, he was asleep, still sitting against the tree.

"Sir," someone said to him. He was still in a deep sleep but could hear the voice. "Excuse me, sir," the voice said again.

Fitz opened his eyes. The Dragon Moon cut shafts of light into the woods. A tall man stood before him; he wore coveralls and a white hard hat. Three other people were standing on each side of the man, one male and two females. One of the females was blonde; the other had red hair. All of them wore hard hats.

"Sir, what would you like us to do?" The tall man asked.

Fitz gave a groggy glance around, "Hmm?"

"We are here to work for you, sir. Anything you need, we will do it."

Fitz thought for a moment, and a smile slowly appeared on his face.

74

When he woke the following day, the landscape had changed. Trees were scattered across the ground; some areas were piles of branches, and some were piles of logs. However, one area had long branches with their pine needle ends spread across the floor of the woods. The branches lay across the ground, strategically entangled into each other. Suddenly, Fitz remembered his dream from the evening before with the workers that appeared before him. He remembered shovels and dirt. He remembered looking down into a massive hole as the workers dug. He remembered helping them as they pulled themselves up to the top of the hole.

He walked to the branches and stepped on them with light pressure. They sagged slightly under his feet. He kneeled and worked his hand through the branches. What should have been solid ground was open air as his hand passed through the branches. He moved his hand around and felt nothing but cool air. He smiled and got back on his feet.

He grabbed his pack and walked, always peeking over his shoulder to ensure the pit was in sight. He found a huge rock stuck out of the ground as high as his head. He crawled onto the rock and lay on his stomach. From this vantage point, he could see the pit.

A day later, he saw four people fall into the pit. Two young boys were leading the way, and as soon as the two adults that followed walked onto the branches, the floor collapsed with a loud set of snaps and crunches, and all four of them dropped out of sight.

Fitz rolled over onto his back and smiled. His eyes gazed up at the canopy above and the blue sky beyond. After a while, he slid off the rock and made a fire. He brewed a cup of tea and topped it off with a splash of whiskey.

When he woke, he stirred the hot coals, started another small fire, and brewed another cup of tea. Then he left his things by the campfire and walked to the pit where four people, whom he had once called his friends, had fallen the previous afternoon. He told them his plans and had to duck away from an arrow shot by Jared.

Then he headed back to his camp with plans to gather his things, hike to the cabin, and kidnap Cambria. When he walked around the massive rock at his campsite, Dorn was standing next to his things.

Chapter 23

After Dorn cleared the Dark Forest, he continued north quickly. He could smell a campfire when he reached the thick part of the woods. He continued to follow the smell and found himself next to a huge rock and a smoldering campfire. Next to the campfire was a sleeping bag and a pack. An empty cup lay on the ground next to the pack, and a sword leaned against the tree. Dorn immediately recognized the sword as Fitz's sword. He grabbed the sword and tossed it into the surrounding foliage.

Dorn knew it wouldn't be long before Fitz returned. Maybe he went on a quick hunt or needed to relieve himself. Dorn wasn't sure. What he was sure of was a fair fight. He pulled his sword from the sheath and tossed it into the tall grass not far from Fitz's sword, then he reached into his leather vest and loosened his dagger from its hiding place. He kept it in its place but just wanted it loose for easy access.

Dorn waited at Fitz's campsite for several minutes. He thought of stoking the fire and making some tea but feared it would sidetrack him. He remained focused and used his senses to monitor all directions.

He heard footsteps approaching and soon could see the top of Fitz's head over the rock at the edge of camp. He took a deep breath and let it out to calm himself as much as possible.

When Fitz walked around the rock and saw Dorn, he had a moment of surprise in his gait, but he recovered with the composure of a seasoned criminal.

"Dorn," he said and smiled. "What brings you to these parts?"

Dorn had been standing with his thumbs tucked in the front pockets of his vest. He glared at Fitz and said, "What do you think?"

Fitz grinned and said, "Let me guess, you found Mylo?"

"And a dead dragon earlier that day," Dorn said.

"Ahh, the dragon," Fitz glanced toward the ground and nodded. Then he looked back at Dorn, "That wasn't me."

"Of course, it wasn't," Dorn said sarcastically as he stepped away from the tree he had been leaning against. "And how should I believe that?"

"You know I'm a straight shooter, Dorn."

"But you've been lying to us for how long? Years?"

Fitz stared at him with his cold eyes.

"Why?" Dorn asked.

"Why not? What was in it for me?" Fitz asked. "Comradery? Helping others?"

Dorn stepped forward and glared at Fitz with his dark eyes. "We all knew that long ago, Fitz. We were all in it together. Helping others as much as we could, and great things were in store."

"None of it sounded that great to me," Fitz said.

"Then why did you stick around?"

Fitz shrugged his shoulders. "I don't know." He pulled his dagger from the sheath on his side and ran the side of the blade along the sharp edge of the rock like he was sharpening it. Then he slipped the blade back into his vest. "Immature, I guess."

"So, what kind of deal did you make?" Dorn asked.

"Land," Fitz said, taking a few steps so that the large rock was now behind him. "Gold. You know, all the good things in life."

"And that carried more weight than the commitment we've all had for one another since our teens."

"Yeah, pretty much."

"I trusted you," a sadness grew over Dorn's eyes. "I would have done anything for you."

Fitz stood without a change of expression.

"So, what now?" Dorn asked.

Fitz jerked his head and said, "Your friends are over yonder stuck in a pit. They will die there." He leaned back against the rock and said, "After I kill you, I will go to the cabin, capture Cambria, and take her to Erikson's Castle. If she doesn't find a cure for Ivan Erickson, she will be put to death."

Before he could continue, Dorn began to walk toward Fitz. His dark eyes were fierce, and his hands were in fists. "Where are they?" Dorn said through gritted teeth.

"Wouldn't you like to know," Fitz said as he met Dorn toe to toe.

Dorn threw a punch at him, but Fitz blocked it and countered with a shot to the jaw that sent Dorn to the ground. Fitz jumped on him, but Dorn pushed his feet into Fitz's chest and sent him flying.

They both regained their stances, and Dorn hit him with two quick punches to the face. When Fitz was arched from the blows, Dorn gave him a hefty punch to the midsection, which caused Fitz to double over. Dorn answered with an uppercut that lifted Fitz off the ground and landed him on his back. Fitz rolled to his side, gasping for air.

Dorn held his stance and waited for Fitz to get to his feet as if he were scrapping with someone in the streets of Ironwood. He would never strike a man on the ground. His hopes of Fitz coming to his senses and giving up faded as soon as Fitz got back to his feet with his dagger in hand. He rushed Dorn and swiped the knife at him, but Dorn jumped out of the way, avoiding any damage.

When they turned and faced each other again, Dorn pulled his dagger and said, "It doesn't have to end like this."

"But it has to end. For all of you." They walked slowly in a circle, their daggers held firmly in their hands.

"That will never happen," Dorn said.

"Yes, it will. For all of Ironwood."

"You don't like the taste of freedom? Because that is what we have on our side of the river."

"The taste of power is so much sweeter," Fitz smiled. His blue eyes were fierce.

"You are such a fool," Dorn said and then went on an attack toward Fitz. He was careful with his footwork as he approached. Fitz backpedaled, and the knife jabs went back and forth, but no blood was drawn or clothes torn. After several steps, Fitz had his back against a large rock. He held his dagger out as Dorn stood firm-footed. Fitz fought like a wolf trapped in a corner; there was no way out, but his backside was protected. His focus was only on what was in front of him. His eyes showed no fear, and his facial expression showed he enjoyed the challenge.

Dorn weighed his options carefully. He was going toe to toe with one of his oldest friends. He had no intentions of killing Fitz, but the progression of the last few moments made him aware that Fitz had no qualms about killing him. Dorn could keep Fitz trapped in a corner for only so long. If he turned away, Fitz would attack. Dorn had no choice but to be the aggressor. In the back of his mind, he remembered where he had tossed his sword.

Dorn drove in for an attack, but Fitz stood his ground. Their daggers swiped at each other, but they only cut the thick air of the woods.

"You really want to do this?" Dorn said as he backed away.

"It's over, Dorn," Fitz said without moving away from the rock behind him.

Dorn backed into the tall grass and kept his eyes on the man he once called a friend. He reached down with both hands and came up with a sword in each. He tossed one to Fitz, who caught it with one hand. "Then we end this the right way. Move away from the rock and fight like a man," Dorn said.

Fitz walked away from the rock and took a stance, ready to fight.

They danced and jabbed for a few minutes. This was no sparring session; this was the real deal. Mistakes could be made and learned from while sparring, but one small mistake would cost one of them their life.

The fight ended up being shorter than either of them thought it would be. Dorn had attacked with his sword with a barrage of swipes while Fitz blocked them. The quick defensive moves put Fitz at a momentary disadvantage, which Dorn capitalized on. Instead of his sword being out before him, Fitz's sword was vertical, exposing his torso and hands.

Dorn swung his sword with both hands and stuck Fitz's hand. The bones in his hand were crushed, and he dropped the sword immediately. Fitz took the pain well, only letting out a grunt. Dorn dropped his sword, pulled his dagger, and leaped toward Fitz. He plunged the knife into his stomach and up into his heart, just the way he had witnessed when his father got murdered. He wrapped his other arm around Fitz's shoulders, embracing him in a hug. He whispered in his ear as Fitz died, "I'm sorry, my friend. I don't know how it came to this, but I am sorry." Then he gently lowered him to the ground.

#

Dorn looked at the ground of the woods carefully. He looked for leaves and grass that were pressed down. Like a hunter looking for the faintest blood trail of its prey, Dorn looked to the ground for a sign of a footstep or something that was dropped. He meticulously worked his way down a trail that only one person had traveled. Every few steps, he glanced up to take in his surroundings. Soon, he saw something peculiar in the landscape of the wood. There was a large hole in the ground. Dorn stopped paying attention to the path that he was following, and minutes later, he was rescuing his friends.

Once they got Billy to the cabin, Dorn went back and dug a shallow grave, placed Fitz's body in it, and after he covered it with dirt, he placed boulders over the grave to keep animals from digging up the body.

After fetching Fitz's sword out of the grass nearby, Dorn stabbed the ground at the head of the grave. The sword stood, and the pommel pointed toward the sky as Dorn stood beside the grave.

He was sad that it had come to this. He had been friends with Fitz for a long time and always trusted him. How all of this had slipped through the cracks, he didn't know. Dorn never suspected anything and was ashamed of himself for not seeing it.

He closed his eyes and tilted his head to the sky. Then he lowered his head, opened his eyes, and walked away from Fitz's grave. He never looked back.

Everything that happened in the last few days made Dorn realize that the feud with Lance had grown more than he had imagined, and it was about to worsen.

Part II: Greystone

Chapter 24

"Wakey, wakey, Billy Blaine."

Billy tried to open his eyes. The voice was familiar, but he was having trouble pinpointing whose it was.

"Billy!"

Billy opened his eyes to a snarling bear just inches from his face. He was startled at first but then recognized it as his headgear. He thought, *I guess you CAN take some of your belongings to the next world.*

As he moved, pain screamed through his body. He sat up with a groan and put the bear's head on his lap.

"Well, well, well," the voice said.

Billy looked up. Lance sat in a chair a few feet away. His dark hair fell alongside his face and draped over his shoulders. Silver jewelry adorned his ears. Lance folded his arms across his chest, revealing tattoos. On one arm was a snake that wound its way down his forearm. The head of the snake rested on his left hand. On his right arm was a sword; the pommel was on the top of his hand, and the blade ran up to his elbow.

"Did you sleep well?" Lance asked sarcastically.

"Where am I?" Billy asked as he grimaced. "Is this the afterlife? What did I do wrong to be with you?"

"Only the privileged will be able to be with me in the afterlife, Billy. Maybe someday you will be so lucky."

"So, where am I?" Billy groaned.

"You fell right out of the In Between and landed at my feet."

"So, I'm not dead?"

"No, Billy," Lance smiled. "I couldn't kill you. At least not in the In Between."

"You sure tried to kill us all," Billy winced in pain and then glared at Lance.

"Oh, humor me, Billy. That wasn't me that tried to kill you all."

"It was your Gods then."

"Oh, well, they have a plan, you know?" Lance tilted his head slightly to the side. "Maybe their plan was for you to be with me."

"That sounds like a horrible plan," Billy said as he held the bear's head closer to his chest.

"Aw," Lance said. "You got your little teddy bear with you?"

"If we are in Evergreen, Dorn and Jared will find me," Billy said.

"Foolish, Billy. You are dead to them. They buried some of your belongings at the base of Rickenback Mountain, with the thought of," Lance giggled. "The thought of you having a smooth transition to the next world," he said, holding his head back and laughing heartily.

"Why are you so condescending?" Billy raised his voice. "You do realize I have lived an entire life. I may be twelve as we sit here, but I have life experiences that accumulated into great wisdom." Billy pointed his finger at Lance. "I can outsmart you, Lance Erikson."

Lance pushed Billy's finger away and said, "Oh, Billy. You are so naïve. Just accept the fact that you are now under my wing. You could even call me 'Dad' or maybe just 'Uncle Lance.' Or maybe we could be brothers."

"Not a chance, Bucko!"

Lance held his hands to his chest, "Oh, you hurt my feelings." Then he leaned forward with his elbows on his knees and shook off the sarcasm. "You are mine, Billy. You will remain here in my castle until you are an old man. If you outlive me, I will ensure my offspring will see to my wishes." Lance stood and said, "Get used to these stone walls." Then he turned and walked away.

Chapter 25

For the first five days, Billy was confined to a small cell. It was cold and dusty; gray stones had been shaped and stacked between rows and columns of mortar that made up the walls. Billy could hear a mouse scurrying under the door and around the cell while he tried to sleep at night. At the top of one wall was a small window with four vertical bars. The window was too high for Billy to be able to see through. Late in the afternoon, the sun blazed through it, but even the rays were too high to warm him on the cold stone floor. He heard voices coming in the window, but nothing was clear enough to decipher.

Twice a day, a guard would give him food through a slot in the heavy wooden door, and the meals were typically bland sandwiches made of dry, grainy bread and molasses. His hunger grew as the days went by.

After the fifth day, a guard took him to a large dormitory. Dozens of beds lined the walls, and a small wooden trunk was at the foot of each one. Each bed had its sheet pulled up nice and neat, just as his mother had taught him when he was a young boy in Detroit. Billy counted over a dozen beds in the dormitory. Wooden sconces that hung on the walls lit the room. There were no windows. He and the guard who escorted him were the only ones there.

The guard walked to one bed and pointed, "You will sleep here. Wake up when the roosters crow. Tomorrow, you will be given your duties."

"Duties?" Billy looked at the guard.

"Yes," the guard said. "Don't ask questions."

"Why not," Billy stuck his nose toward the guard.

The guard smacked him in the face, "That's why." Then, the guard turned and walked away.

Billy watched the guard go and rubbed his stinging cheek. He sat on his mattress momentarily, then stood up and went to the wooden trunk at the end of his bed. He opened it, but the only things inside were a bar of soap and a towel.

Later in the day, children began to file into the dormitory. There was minimal talk among the kids. A boy sat on a bed to Billy's right, a girl to his left.

The boy looked at him, "What's your name?" The boy had a heavy English accent. His hair was red, and freckles littered his pale face.

"Billy," he said.

"I'm Jack."

Billy stuck his hand out. The boy looked at it for a moment, and just when Billy was about to take it back, the boy shook it. "It's nice to meet you," Billy said.

"That's Orla," Jack pointed.

A girl waved to him without a word. She had blonde hair and green eyes.

Billy waved back and looked at the boy, "How long have you been here?"

Jack shrugged his shoulders.

"What do you do here?" Billy asked.

"Work," Jack said.

"Sometimes it's really hard work," the girl said. Her voice was scratchy.

"How often do you go home?" Billy asked.

"Never," both of his neighbors said in unison.

"Listen up!" a voice bellowed. The children looked to the end of the room. A man with blonde hair walked from the door and looked around as he slowly paced. A sword hung from the man's side, and his boots clicked on the stone floor.

"I've seen him before," Billy whispered.

Jack gave him an alert look.

The man walked to Billy's bed and stopped. "We have a new resident. His name is Billy," the man smirked at Billy. "Tomorrow, Billy will start with his new duties." The man chuckled for a moment. "Chamber pots!"

Jack's head dropped, and he looked at the floor.

"If Billy doesn't do his job well, the rest of you will pay," he said. "Is that understood?

"Yes, Boris," all the children, except Billy, said in unison.

"Some of you will go to town with me in four days. If you see your parents, you will tell them how wonderful it is here. Is that correct?"

"Yes, Boris."

Chapter 26

Chamber pot duty was horrible. Billy gagged at the stench the moment he entered the room. A large metal tub sat on rollers underneath a chute. The chute was where all the castle's waste pipes came together. Human waste tumbled out of the chute occasionally, plopping into the tub.

Once the tub was three-quarters full, Billy had to wheel it down the tracks on which it rode. When the tub was over the pit, he tilted it on its hinges and dumped it. He then rinsed the tub with water. Down below in the pit, a large paddle churned the waste. Billy would find out later that, in a stream outside the castle, a water wheel powered the paddle. The water wheel spun, transferring energy through gears and poles, which caused the paddles to turn in the water below. He would also learn that the waste soup that resulted was used on the local crops for fertilizer. Billy nearly retched at the thought.

For several days, he continued to do the same job. He worked alone, and his only conversation was with Jack and Orla in the evenings. Knowing that the children's daily work in the castle was a group effort, Billy learned to keep quiet. The entire group paid the price if one person failed to do their job correctly or had a disciplinary episode.

Punishments ranged from no dinner to sleeping in one of the cells on the concrete floor. The perpetrator got to choose who would be punished that day. That child was forced to select four or five other children to sleep in the cells. Then, the perpetrator was invited to eat with the guardsmen, which typically consisted of a hearty five-course meal. The guardsmen ate well, so this was the worst punishment possible, being forced to eat a healthy meal while five of your friends slept on a cold concrete floor with no blankets, and the rest of the children went to bed with no dinner. It was a position no child in Erikson's castle wished to be in.

This odd punishment forced the children to look out for one another and stick together. This union played them right into Lance's hands. He controlled the children as a collective. When it came time to build an army, Lance would have an obedient group that would be easy to train.

Billy sensed this after only a few weeks at the castle. He knew Lance was playing all of them into his hands.

Chapter 27

Billy went from chamber pot duty to kitchen duty. He helped prep food for the guardsmen and the children. He shucked sweet corn, washed vegetables, peeled carrots and potatoes, and prepared meats with various seasonings; after the food was prepared, he washed all the utensils and cleaned off the granite countertops.

When he finished his kitchen duties in the evening, he and the others could often roam the courtyard as long as nobody had caused trouble that day. A few times a week, Boris or Lance would lead a group of children in exercises that dealt with swords, daggers, and hand-to-hand fighting. Billy had no desire to be a part of these groups or to learn to fight with a sword, although he did admire Dorn and Raistlin for their talents with steel. Ultimately, he had no will to hurt or kill anyone. Deep inside, he knew that these children were getting trained to fight against the people of Ironwood and possibly against the people of Greystone if there was ever an uprising. Billy had read enough history books to know that Lance, in tandem with some of the crazy dictators throughout history, was both a lunatic and a genius. His ducks were in a row; he was prepared. Although his army was young, they would be the most significant force in Evergreen in a few years.

Chapter 28

Across the river, the people of Ironwood went about their business nonchalantly; their most significant concerns were harvesting a good crop and attending to the needs of their neighbors. They were unaware of the force being built on the other side of the river outside the village. Billy had heard Dorn mention gathering men and building a force, but Raistlin was too passive to allow it to happen with more than a few volunteers. Billy knew that if Dorn, Raistlin, and Jared ever returned to Evergreen, Raistlin would not live long. With Raistlin gone and Jared's knowledge of war tactics, maybe Dorn's willingness to fight would prepare them for a battle. Billy knew it wouldn't be enough.

There was no longer a neighborly tiff between Dominic Hale and Ivan Erikson; Lance had taken the reins and planned to prove who Evergreen's leader would be. If Lance had it his way, there would be absolute bloodshed.

The thought made Billy cringe. Many nights, he lie awake with thoughts running through his head. He needed to find a way to Ironwood and the Barrow Homestead but knew escaping the castle grounds would be nearly impossible. Even if he did, his new friends would be punished. If Billy never returned to the castle grounds, he would always wonder how his friends fared after his escape. Billy Blaine was much too empathetic to do such a thing.

He needed a conduit to the outside, a bird, a messenger, something.

Chapter 29

Billy first saw Teagan while working in the kitchen. Boris came through the door, and Teagan followed. Boris barked out orders and laid out a timetable for the food to be finished. Most of the children, a year or two older than Billy, shuffled quickly around the kitchen after the orders were given.

Teagan was intimidating with his broad chest and tattooed arms. His brown hair fell to his shoulders and partially into his face. He scanned the room; his eyes stopped on Billy momentarily, then moved on. After a moment, he followed Boris out the door.

"Who was that?" Billy leaned over to Mei. He met Mei when he first started working in the kitchen. At first, he was taken aback by her beauty. She was a little older than he. She had long dark hair that was always in a ponytail when they worked in the kitchen, but when he saw her in the dormitory or outside, her hair fell over her shoulders. Her wide-set eyes were dark, and a thin nose accentuated her light skinned face. Her lips were beautiful as well, although she rarely smiled. From the day they met, Mei and Billy became fast friends.

"The dark haired guy?" She looked at Billy. They were paired up for a time to shuck corn and then boil it. "That's Teagan."

"What's he like?" Billy asked.

"Teagan?" Mei paused as she looked at the door the men had just exited. "He looks mean and may act like it when he is with Boris or one of the guardsmen. But, honestly, he is nice when it is just him. He has come into the kitchen by himself and talked with us."

#

The next day, Teagan walked into the kitchen while everyone prepared dinner. His arms stuck out of a leather vest and crossed over his chest. He was intimidating but often smiled after mentioning something to one of the kids.

He walked to Billy and said, "Hi."

Billy glanced at him and returned the greeting.

"You're new here," Teagan said.

Billy nodded and said, "Yes. Sir."

"What's your name?" Teagan asked without a smile.

"My name's Billy, Billy Blaine," Billy said.

Teagan nodded. They didn't participate in a handshake. "How long have you been here?"

"It's been a few weeks," Billy said. "They had me on chamber pots for a while."

Teagan gave a winced look, "That's a bummer." He began to walk away, then stopped and turned to Billy. "You look familiar."

Billy shrugged his shoulders.

"Are you from Greystone?" Teagan asked.

Billy shook his head.

"Hmm," Teagan said. "I swear I've seen you before."

#

That night, Teagan sat up after looking at the stars. There were only a few hours left before he and Sky had to go their ways to avoid getting caught together.

They had spent the night under a copse of trees outside the castle walls, huddled together under a blanket.

"That's where I remember him," Teagan said.

Sky reached up and touched his arm, "Who?" She said with a groggy voice.

"Billy, the boy I met today," Teagan said. He shifted his body so he was facing her. "Remember I told you about the sword fight that Lance was in at the foot of the castle? Billy was there. That's where I have seen him before. I know it was him."

#

The next evening, Teagan walked through the courtyard to an area near Billy's bench. A stone knee wall surrounded the courtyard. The benches and tables were arranged around the perimeter of the courtyard, near the knee wall.

"Are your duties done for today?" Teagan said in a gruff voice.

"Yes, sir," Billy said, then stood as a sign of respect.

"Sit down, Billy," Teagan said in a quieter voice than before. "How do I know you?"

Billy sat, shrugged his shoulders, and looked up at Teagan. Once he realized Teagan wasn't looking at him, he said, "I don't know."

"Where are you from?" Teagan said as he gazed at the perimeter walls in the distance.

Billy opened his mouth for a moment, then closed it. He looked up at Teagan and said, "Ironwood, no, wait!" he paused, then said, "Barrow Homestead." Billy immediately dropped his head after giving the information. He felt he had already told this man too much and may have been falling into a trap.

"So, you know Raistlin Barrow," Teagan said, not stating it as a question.

Billy continued to sit without looking up.

"Listen," Teagan said as he gazed to the side. "You were here with another boy your age. Raistlin fought with Lance at the base of the castle." Teagan looked to where the fight had taken place, pointed, and said, "Right over there."

Billy turned his head toward Teagan but didn't look up. Billy realized that Teagan was trying to keep their conversation unnoticed. For all someone in the distance knew, Teagan could have been talking to himself since he was looking at no one in particular while he spoke.

"The man that was with all of you was killed," Teagan said.

Billy looked up momentarily, then turned his attention back to the ground.

"Dorn and a young woman came for him, but the rest of you disappeared," Teagan said. "Where did you go?"

Billy kept silent.

"So, I have meetings with Dorn Hale at a saloon in Ironwood every few days. He is married to the mayor."

Billy glanced up at Teagan.

"What would you like me to tell him, Billy?" Teagan asked.

Billy looked off to the side without a word.

"Fair enough," Teagan said, pulling his foot off the bench and standing tall. "I will get your trust, Billy. Everything is at stake. You will learn to trust me." Teagan turned and began to walk away.

Billy turned his head, looked toward Teagan, and said, "Raistlin lived in Detroit in my old world before he came back to Evergreen. Ask Dorn the name of Raistlin's dog. If you come back with the right answer, then I will trust you."

Teagan stopped momentarily but did not turn around, and then he continued walking.

Chapter 30

Mei, Orla, Jack, and Billy spent much of their spare time together. Once Mei and Billy finished kitchen duty, they often caught up with Jack and Orla. Jack's days consisted of tending to the garden, whether picking carrots and muskmelon or turning the ground with a plow pulled behind a horse.

Every third evening, Jack trained with the older children on sword fighting techniques. Lance or Boris usually led the training. Occasionally, Brenna led the training when the others were out on a hunting expedition.

Orla was on stable duty. The work was non-stop, day after day. She cleaned the stables, brushed the horses, fed the big beasts, and led them out into the pasture; she and two other teenagers did whatever needed doing in the stables. Orla had a close call early on during her stable duty. She walked behind a horse without putting her hand on its rump. The horse kicked her and sent her flying. Her calf was bruised so badly that she couldn't walk on it for days.

#

As the days went on, the conversations grew more profound.

"Mei," Billy said. "How did you end up in Evergreen? You said you don't have parents here."

Mei glanced up at him from her empty plate. She and Billy were always part of the last group to finish dinner, as they were responsible for preparing the food. Her brown eyes were glassy, and tears welled up; her long eyelashes fluttered up and down with each blink.

Billy nodded and touched her hand for a moment.

#

Later in the evening, Mei confided in Billy under the light of the sconces at the castle's base.

"There was a war," she said. A tear escaped her eye. "Our city was bombed; we were running from our neighborhood, so many houses were on fire. Dozens of planes flew overhead and dropped bomb after bomb. The planes seemed to come nonstop, over and over. Soon, it seemed that everything was on fire." She wiped her cheek and looked away from Billy while they sat on the stone bench. "I saw a door as we ran down an empty street. It was a door I had never seen on a street I knew well." She sobbed for a moment, then regained her composure. "I pulled at my mother's hand to go to the door. She told me to run while my father looked to the sky. I ran to the door, and when I crawled through it, it shut, and I was separated from my parents." She wiped the tears from her cheeks. "I haven't seen them since." She dropped her head to her hands and continued to cry.

Billy leaned to her and hugged her. "Is that when you came here?"

She shook her head, "No. I was in another world with a variety of tunnels. I didn't know where to go." She wiped more tears with her sleeve.

"Where were you from?" Billy asked. "Do you remember the year?"

"I was born in Japan," Mei said. "I was born in 1933."

"What happened in the world of tunnels?" Billy asked.

Mei hesitated momentarily, "I searched but wasn't sure where to go. Other children were doing all kinds of fun things. I walked through tunnel after tunnel, but I had no idea where I was. As evening approached, Lance walked up to me.

He was charming and nice and said he would help me find my way home. Then I ended up here. I have seen him but haven't talked to him since. He acts like I don't exist." She looked Billy in the eyes. "It was obvious that helping me was not in his best interest."

"No," Billy said. "No, it isn't."

#

Billy learned that Jack was also a victim of the same war as Mei, albeit on the other side of the world. He and his family were trying to survive in Nazi Germany. They were gathered with many people from the community in a neighbor's basement during a bombing run. As bombs flashed in the small basement windows and the walls of the house shook, a small door appeared on the wall of the basement. Jack's father was the only person in the room that saw it appear. It was a small wooden door shaped like an arch. He grabbed Jack and told him to go through. Jack was apprehensive, but his father convinced him and said he would follow. Once Jack ducked through the door, it slammed shut and disappeared. He also found himself in a world with a labyrinth of tunnels and experienced the same fear and confusion that Mei did, and Lance showed up pretending to be the hero.

They sat on stone benches around a small table with a flame emanating from its center. Orla told them in her scratchy voice that she was born in Greystone, but her parents often talked about another life they had lived elsewhere. One night, a group of people from Erikson's castle banged on the door and pushed her father aside when he opened it. Before she knew it, she was swept away and taken to the castle. Her only interactions with her parents since were the rare trips to town with Lance, Boris, or Brenna. During these trips, she was only allowed to wave to her parents. Anything beyond that was prohibited.

Chapter 31

Lance's crew sat at the mahogany table for their weekly dinner together. Lance sat at the head of the table. Brenna sat at the other end. Teagan, Boris, and two more of Lance's elite filled out the sides.

Serving trays of roasted chicken, sweet potatoes, snow peas, and Scotch eggs sat on the table. Warm rolls sat in small wire baskets lined with cloth. Their goblets were filled with honey mead.

Once their plates were stacked with food, Boris held his goblet in the air and said, "Let's have a toast to Lance and Brenna for their safe trip back to Evergreen."

They cheerfully raised their drinks, sipped the mead, and ate. They pulled at the chicken meat with their fingers, and before they knew it, they were refilling their goblets.

Teagan wiped his beard and said, "How was your trip, Lance?"

Lance held a piece of chicken in his hand. His face glowed from the light of the candles on the table. "We had a great time." Then he looked across the table at Brenna and winked. "We were transformed into wolves for a few moments. And we ruined the life of one of the Collins brothers."

"Who are the Collins?" Teagan asked.

Lance wiped his mouth with his cloth napkin and said, "The Collins are a family from the other world. Those two brothers and Billy Blaine messed everything up for me. Any trip to the other world is risky. You may never find a door back to Evergreen." He took a sip of mead and went on, "But these three could dance between worlds. They never should have made it to Evergreen, but now they always have the Great Fathers helping them," Lance rolled his eyes. "It amazes me how such peons can ruin my day."

"I've met Billy," Teagan said.

Lance turned to him, "Of course you have. How are his kitchen duties?"

"Great," Teagan said, hustling some peas around his plate. His hair fell into his eyes. "He doesn't complain. He does what he is told."

Lance rested his hands on the arms of his chair, "Of course he does." He leaned back and looked toward the ceiling of the chamber.

When the dinner was finished and everyone was excused, Boris stopped Teagan in the hallway. "You ask a lot of questions," he said.

"I just like to be informed," Teagan smiled and crossed his tattooed arms.

"You just seem a little too nosy," Boris said.

Teagen shook his head. "Jealousy will get you nowhere, my friend."

"We're not friends."

Teagan chuckled and, with a hint of sarcasm, said, "Oh, we're not? Ah! I forgot!" He leaned forward and said, "I got the girl." Then he spun on his heel and walked out of the castle.

Boris fumed as he watched him go.

Chapter 32

"Atticus."

Billy heard the word but thought nothing of it as he helped Jack pull weeds in the castle garden. Billy was on one side of the long garden, Jack on the other.

"Atticus is the name of the dog," the voice said.

Billy lifted his head and looked toward the sound of the voice. Teagan stood at the edge of the courtyard cobblestones and looked out at the perimeter walls. Billy continued to look at Teagan but said nothing as he pulled weeds.

Teagan looked at Billy and nodded.

Billy stood and glanced at Jack, who kept pulling weeds as if nothing else was happening. Then Billy looked back at Teagan.

"He told me Raistlin had a dog, and his name was Atticus," Teagan said.

Billy stopped pulling weeds and was about to speak, then Teagan said, "He wanted me to ask you something. Something to cement his trust in me."

"Go on," Billy said.

"He wanted me to ask you what he said when you two were under the stars after the balloon ride."

Billy thought for a moment, "He said, We'll be fine," he paused, "We'll be fine, as long as we're under the same sky."

Teagan looked out at the trees beyond the perimeter walls. If others were watching, they wouldn't know he was speaking with Billy. "Mr. Blaine, I think we can be friends. I am going to meet with your friend Dorn in a few days. We have some things to talk about."

Although Teagan wasn't looking at him, Billy nodded and returned to pulling weeds. Across the garden, Jack went about his business, oblivious to the exchange that had just happened.

Chapter 33

Billy, Mei, Orla, and Jack usually gathered in the courtyard and played games like marbles or hacky sack, the latter being played by kicking a little footbag around in a circle. It was a game that Billy's daughter loved to play when he lived in the other world. When they stayed inside the castle during these times, they would sit in a circle under one of the bunks and play card games like Go Fish or War. Both games were familiar in Evergreen amongst children. Card playing was popular in the saloons, both in Greystone and Ironwood. The most popular card games were Brag and Boston. Many of the saloon fights stemmed from disagreements that arose during these games.

When the four children played, there were rarely disagreements. Often, the games were overshadowed by stories from their lives before they were forced to live in Erikson's castle.

"What was life like when you still lived in town with your parents?" Billy asked Orla.

"I had fun with my friends, playing games like this under the shade of a willow," she said. Billy leaned forward while she spoke. Her hoarse and raspy voice was often hard to hear. "But life was scary."

"How so?" Billy asked.

"There were times I was at my daddy's bakery when men from the castle came in. They usually took half of the money he had in the shop." She looked at Billy and asked, "Do you have a nine?"

"Go fish."

She drew a card from the pile and continued, "Then they would take most of the bread he had baked that day. They called it a tax. They said it was for the town's good, but the town never got better. Everyone was poor. Daddy would come home with two loaves of bread, and that was dinner with some vegetables that Momma had pulled from the garden. The castle took so much money from us that we hardly ever had money to buy meat."

"Financial manipulation," Billy said quietly.

"What?" Orla said.

"It's financial manipulation," Billy said. "I remember a movie I watched in my world where a guy pretty much controlled the entire town. He was rich and hired his cronies to work for him. His hired hands would go to the businesses in town and take what they wanted, including cash from the registers and safes. What you told me is the same as this movie; Lance didn't need the money or the food. He took it, so your father had to work harder to restock his bakery. He took his money and product, leaving him no choice but to work harder to return to his previous position. Then Lance and his weasels would return and do it all over again. It's an evil concept, but it works on those who can barely get by. He probably controlled any business owner he did that to in town. Orla, your family is probably only one of the many families he has done this to."

As the evening wore on, Billy learned why Orla's voice was always scratchy. She had developed an infection in her throat, but the doctor in Greystone wasn't very good. He didn't know what caused the ailment and had no medication to fight it. Eventually, the infection disappeared, and Orla's voice had been like that since.

Then the sconces were dimmed, the conversation came to an end, and the cards were put away.

Chapter 34

Neither Lance nor Ivan Erikson were adventurers. Their focus was never on what was on the other side of a mountain or where a river would lead them. Their concern was power over the things that surrounded them. Power and greed fueled the fire within the family for generations, but their greed only went so far. Although it was never admitted, there was a fear of biting off more than they could chew. They felt that exploring outside their reach would weaken their power, so they stuck with what was before them. They ruled the town and owned all of the land to the Snake River. The Eriksons never cared for any of the land beyond. The good hunting and farmland were on the Greystone side of the river.

Before the murder of Dominic Hale, the people of both towns mingled freely across the bridge. Once Ivan Erickson murdered Dominic Hale, things began to change. Women from opposing towns would glare at each other when they shopped. There were often fights in either the saloon in Greystone or the one in Ironwood. As time passed, the people seemed to gravitate toward their towns; mingling on the other side of the river became increasingly less ideal. The final straw was when it was agreed to have Dorn Hale and Lance Erikson, both teenagers at the time, fight without weapons on the center of the bridge that spanned the Snake River. The people of both towns lined the river banks to watch the battle. The bloodied teens wound up tumbling off the bridge and into the river, where they continued to pummel each other.

The fight was considered a draw, and it took both boys weeks to fully recover. That was when the line was drawn. Ivan Erikson prohibited anyone from crossing the bridge, so the residents of Ironwood didn't dare go to Greystone.

#

Teagan knew the history of the families and the towns, and once he started seeing the atrocities happening on his side of the river, he longed for the freedom of Ironwood. If he had moved to Ironwood, it would do nothing for the people of Greystone. He always felt he had to do something to benefit the town, not just himself.

Teagan and Sky sat with their backs against the stone wall that lined the castle's perimeter. Before them was the rocky terrain that led up the small mountain. To the left of them was the two-hundred-foot sheer rock wall.

"I have a plan," he said to Sky as they hunkered under a blanket.

Her blue eyes glanced at him, "What's your plan?"

"I've talked with Dorn Hale more than just a few times."

Sky perked her head up, "Dorn Hale?" She shifted so she was facing Teagan. "Dorn Hale, the legend?"

Teagan nodded.

"So, what does he have to do with this?"

"There is a boy here in the castle; his name is Billy." Teagan glanced around Sky to ensure no one had ventured beyond the back gate. "He is a close friend of Dorn."

"How?"

"It is a long story, but the connection between Dorn and Billy has allowed Dorn to trust me."

"So, what now?"

"I have to rally the townspeople. I have to convince them that we can revolt and they can get their children back." He paused momentarily, then said, "And I'll try to get Dorn Hale to help us."

Chapter 35

"Why were children taken from their homes?" Mei asked Billy.

Billy took a bite of salted beef he had kept in his pocket as a leftover from the evening dinner. He chewed briefly, then said, "Because Lance is a lunatic."

"We know that," Mei said. "But why?"

"He wants to build a force. You see it out in the courtyard." Billy held his hand toward the open area behind the castle, although no training was happening. "He is training fighters." He offered Mei a small piece of meat and continued after she took it, "I think he wants to extend his reach into Ironwood and some of the land beyond."

"Is this just a show of power?" Mei asked.

Billy took a deep breath and said, "Lance is insecure. He tries to do whatever he can to hide those insecurities. He walks and talks a big game but needs others around him to make decisions."

"How do you know this?"

Billy glanced up at the castle towers, "I have friends here in Evergreen that have known Lance since they were kids. I can read him like a book between hearing their stories and my experiences with Lance."

"How many children do you think he has taken?"

"There are dozens here, and I doubt many came of their own free will."

Part III: Wendell Pond

Chapter 36

"Hello, Samira," Laura said, answering her cell phone.

"Hi, Mrs. Collins," Samira said quietly. "You and Daniel should come back up here."

"What is it?"

"It's Josh; they have to amputate," Samira said in a sob.

An errant bus struck Josh Collins near the riverwalk in Detroit in a crazy sequence of events that included an attack by wolves on the Airedale Terrier that Samira was dogsitting. Josh was in a coma, and his broken leg had developed an infection. The infection was spreading, and the only answer the doctors could give was to amputate his leg just above the knee.

Samira, Josh's girlfriend, had talked to the veterinarian a day earlier about Atticus, the dog involved in the scrap with the wolves.

"How is he?" She asked as she put her hands on the counter.

"Well," the veterinarian said. "He was beat up pretty bad." She clicked her pen and slid it into her breast pocket. She folded her arms and looked at Samira, "He has a broken shoulder, and we had to stitch him up in many places. So, he will have a lot of bald spots when you see him." The vet smiled. "We don't think he has any internal damage though."

"Oh, thank God," Samira whispered. "Can I see him?"

"Of course," the vet said. "Come with me." The doctor led Samira down the hallway. "We'd like to keep him overnight again to be sure he is okay." The vet continued to talk as they walked. "You said wolves attacked him?"

Samira nodded.

"Was this reported to the authorities?"

"No," Samira said. "But I don't think the wolves will be coming back."

Chapter 37

"Why is Josh in so much pain if you can't find anything wrong with him?" Jared asked as he sat across the table from Cambria.

She looked up at him; a lock of curly hair was hanging before her face. "I don't know," she said, then looked down at her task. "Maybe he is not completely in our world yet."

Jared reached out, touched her hand, and said, "Wait, what do you mean?"

She looked at him and squeezed his hand, "Your brother may be drifting between worlds." She pulled the lock of hair from her face and tucked it behind her ear. "Josh may still be alive in your world."

"What?" Jared whispered.

Cambria pulled his hand up and kissed it, "It's the only thing that makes sense. I've checked him repeatedly but can't figure out what pains him."

"So, he might live? I mean, in my world? My old world?"

"Maybe."

On the bad days, Cambria made Josh a chamomile tea with a touch of slumber sand. He would spend the day wandering in a daze or sleeping away the afternoon.

Chapter 38

Dorn walked in and leaned his sword and sheath in the corner before he walked to the table. He looked down at the bowl and book between Jared and Cambria. Cambria had been flipping through a dusty, leatherbound book and mixing concoctions for a day and a half.

"I may have it figured out," She looked at Dorn, then at Jared. "I need a mouse."

"A mouse?" Jared asked.

Cambria nodded.

"A mouse?" Dorn asked.

Cambria looked back at him, "A mouse."

Dorn and Jared looked at each other. "Okay," Dorn said.

#

The morning air was damp and misty. The smell of the constant decomposing leaves lingered heavier than usual. What they thought would be a simple hunt for a small rodent ended up being a comedic event of tearing through a wood pile, often seeing a mouse scurry away in fear. Once the top logs were strewn aside, the ones below were mossy and slippery. At one point, Jared stumbled over the pile of logs and rolled onto his back, laughing. A few mice escaped the chaos by sneaking under the leaves and into the tall grass. They leaped at the ones they saw running away and turned their heads toward the ones that rustled the leaves during their escape. They reached the bottom of the pile and blocked in a few of the mice with logs. Once they had a mouse secure in Dorn's satchel, they began to walk back to the house.

Jared looked around and said, "I'm glad nobody saw all that."

"Agreed," Dorn said and let out a huge belly laugh.

Once back inside the house, Dorn held out the satchel, "Do you need it now?"

Cambria nodded and took the satchel from him. "I think I have it. You should both sit down."

Both men sat and watched. The bowl on the table was full of cloudy fluid. Cambria sprinkled a pinch of powder from a small vial into the bowl. She untied the satchel and reached her hand inside. The satchel moved as the mouse wiggled around to avoid Cambria's hand. She pulled the mouse out and held it by its tail as it squeaked and wiggled. She held the mouse over the bowl, then slowly lowered it into the liquid. The mouse moved and splashed as it entered the gray concoction. Cambria held the mouse by the tail as she grabbed a wooden spoon, pushed it underwater, and let go of its tail. She held the spoon in place for a moment and then released it. The spoon floated on top of the liquid, and its handle rested on the rim of the bowl.

Jared and Dorn both gave her a questioning look. Cambria didn't notice the looks as she focused on the bowl before her. The three of them sat silently as the moments passed. Bubbles began to rise from under the spoon, and then the mouse appeared from under the surface. The mouse was much smaller than before Cambria placed it in the liquid. The spoon tilted in the dish as the mouse climbed onto it. The adult mouse that had just been submerged in the liquid was now a baby. It circled the spoon's rim, then quickly ran up the handle and onto the edge of the dish, squeaking along the way. Its squeaks were higher than when Cambria had pulled it from the sack. The mouse, soaked and wet, looked back and forth, then scurried around the dish, stepped down onto the open page of the book, and ran down the page and onto the oak table. Tiny wet prints were left behind on the page; a streak from its tail separated the left prints from the right ones. It ran to the edge of the table, down the leg, and disappeared into the wood bin in the corner of the cabin.

"What just happened?" Jared asked.

Cambria looked at Jared and Dorn and said, "We need to take Daddy to Wendell Pond."

Chapter 39

Jared and Cambria left hours before the sun appeared on the horizon the following day. They rode off quietly under the purple hue of the Traveler's Moon. The leather bags draped over the horses held roots, twigs, seeds, and powders. Their food for the day was also packed away.

Cambria had stayed up all night doing calculations. The difference between a concoction in a small wooden bowl and a small pond was enormous. When they reached the pond, Jared lit an oil lantern and hung it from a low branch of a Yew at the pond's edge.

They gathered firewood, and as Jared struck flint together, Cambria gazed out at the pond as far as the lantern would allow.

Once the fire was lit, Cambria began shaving Orris root and Roseroot into small piles on birch bark. Jared pulled a metal bowl from the pack and began to heat water from the pond. He tossed a few more logs on the fire, and sparks floated before a backdrop of pre-dawn glow.

Once the water began to steam, Cambria sprinkled some of the root shavings into the bowl.

"Why do you have to heat the water when it will all go in the pond?" Jared asked.

Cambria glanced at him, "It helps absorb the medicine from the roots. When it is ready, the roots you see in the water are useless because everything we need has been pulled from them."

"This is like middle school chemistry."

She smiled at him, "I've been doing this for as long as I can remember."

"How did you learn?"

"Daddy taught me about trees and bushes, and I read books that he acquired," She paused for a moment. "That he acquired from your world." She paused again, then said, "From your old world." She grabbed another root and began shaving it. "First, it was cookbooks, but I grew tired of them. Your modern world has more things readily available than my primitive one. A good example was trying to make use of the cookbooks. My world doesn't have the seasonings that modern cooking requires in your world; if those seasonings are here, they haven't been discovered yet. Then he found a few books about home remedies, one of which was titled 'Home Remedies In Your Own Garden.' After reading that one, I became hooked. I think the first thing I made was a salve that you could put on a cut, and after a few uses, it proved that the cuts healed faster and left less of a scar."

"He has been there often? The other world, I mean," Jared asked.

"He has been quite the traveler, even before I was born."

As Cambria continued to tweak her recipe, Jared stacked a few small logs on each side of the fire and set a grate over the burning logs. He put a pan on the grate and checked the warmth of the pan by passing his hand over the top of it every minute or so. Once satisfied, he spread a hunk of lard across the pan, and it popped and sizzled. He cracked four eggs one at a time and drained their contents. He laid two thick slices of bacon next to the spattering eggs. Then he pulled two biscuits from a satchel at his side and set them on the edges of the grate.

"Where did you get the biscuits?" Cambria asked.

"Your mother snuck them to me when you were busy last night."

Cambria smiled, "Of course she did."

When the food was to their satisfaction, they cut their biscuits in half, placed their eggs and bacon in the middle, and made breakfast sandwiches. After two bites, Cambria wiped her sandwich across the pan and soaked up some bacon-flavored lard.

She looked at Jared, said, "Why not?" and took a bite.

He grinned and said, "Monkey see, monkey do." He also wiped his sandwich across the pan and took a bite.

After they finished their breakfast, they sat with their backs to the fire, gazing at the sky. The colors changed by the moment; streaks of different shades of blue and yellow shot up from the horizon. The birds sang as the sky brightened.

Cambria and Jared sat cross-legged on the ground, their hands clasped.

"I love you," Jared said.

"I love you," Cambria said. Neither of them took their gaze from the everchanging horizon.

"Is this going to work?" Jared whispered.

"Great Fathers, I hope so," she whispered back.

When the sun broke over the horizon, it was like an egg with the top cracked open, but instead of a chick's beak pipping out of the shell, a burst of light came out and shot into the sky. The top edges of the sun glowed like a small golden hill in the distance, engulfed in flames so bright that one would shade their eyes when looking. The sky changed colors from dark purple to pink to dark blue. Minute by minute, the flaming hill grew bigger and bigger. Soon, all the colors of the morning dawn burned away to a cloudless blue sky.

Once the sun was over the horizon, Cambria stood up and brushed the dry grass from her day dress; her curly hair fell into her face as she leaned over. With one hand, she brushed the hair back; the other, she held out to Jared and said, "C'mon, we have work to do."

Chapter 40

After a breakfast of biscuits, gravy, bacon, and toast with raspberry jam, Dorn and Anastasia readied the wagon with blankets and pillows. Sally harnessed Goldie and hitched her to the front. They gathered their things: food, a small amount of firewood, medicine for Raistlin and Josh, a jug of fresh water, and a change of clothes for Raistlin.

Sally and Dorn helped Raistlin out of the house and to the wagon. It took both of them to support him as he tried to walk. Josh limped close behind. He grimaced with every step.

Once they reached the wagon, they helped Raistlin onto the back of it. He crawled onto the blankets and laid his head on one of the pillows. He fell asleep immediately.

"Josh," Dorn said. "You should ride in the back with him."

Josh nodded and climbed on.

Tessa and Nana rode on the wagon seat with Anastasia squeezed between them. Sawyer bounced away on Anastasia's lap. Two fingers of one hand were in his mouth; the other hand waved erratically toward the treetops. Raistlin slept in the back on the pile of blankets while Josh sat up and watched the scenery before them. Dorn and Sally walked before Goldie; Sally led her with the reins. With every bump and divot in the dusty road, Josh gritted his teeth to the phantom pains in his leg.

They took their time as they traveled. They took the road past Rickenback Mountain, and the trees thickened as they neared the Snake River. Once they could hear the sound of the river, they turned right onto a less-traveled path that was mainly overgrown with weeds. The weeds scraped the bottom of the wagon as they went. The trees began to thin out as they moved farther away from the river. The river banks were heavy with weeping willows, but now it was more cyprus and fir. If one had their eyes closed during the entire ride, they would still be able to detect the transition in the tree species by the smell. Before, it was pollen and leaves; now, it was pine with citrus.

Soon, they saw two horses hitched to trees before the pond. They stopped the wagon, and Sally unhooked Goldie from the reins. Jared approached them with a smile. He reached up and took Sawyer from Anastasia.

"Hey, little buddy," he said, kissing his son on the forehead. He held Sawyer with one arm, then put out his free hand to help Tessa and Anastasia from the wagon. Dorn helped Nana from the other side.

Sally began to walk Goldie toward the pond, then Jared said, "Sally."

Sally turned to look at him.

"The horses can't drink from the pond today. Cambria's got all kinds of stuff going on in the water."

"Ah," she nodded. "I'll take her down to the stream."

"I'll grab the other two and catch up," Dorn said as he headed toward the horses that Jared and Cambria rode on earlier that morning. He untied both of them and followed Sally and Goldie to the stream.

Jared walked to the fire and came back with a cup. A tiny amount of steam came rolling off the top.

"Here," he held it out to Josh with his free hand. "Cambria made it for you."

Josh slid off the back of the wagon and took the cup, "She is very kind."

"She said it's not too strong. She didn't want to knock you out today. She wants us all to be here and aware."

"What's the occasion?" Josh asked.

Jared looked at the pond, "You'll see."

Jared walked to a satchel near the fire and pulled out a hatchet. He slid the hatchet into a leather loop on his belt. He set Sawyer on the ground and helped him balance on his feet.

"Go to Grandma," he said. "Daddy's going to get some firewood."

Tessa stooped just a few yards from him and held out her arms, "C'mon, Sawyer!"

The toddler made a gallant effort to make the long trek to Grandma but went down in a small cloud of dust before he was halfway there. He worked himself back to his feet in a fit of tears, but they were tears of frustration more than pain. On his second attempt, he reached Tessa's grasp and celebrated with a laugh.

"I'll go with you, Jare," Josh said as he sipped the tea Cambria had made him. He went to set the cup on the back of the wagon but then decided to take it with him.

The brothers walked toward a more densely wooded area, and Jared began pulling fallen branches from the brush. Some of them he hacked in half with his hatchet for easier carrying.

When Josh finished his cup of medicine, his limp almost disappeared. He unbuckled his belt, fished it through the handle of the cup, and buckled back up with the cup hanging at his side.

"Why does my leg always hurt so bad, but Cambria can't find anything wrong with it?" Josh asked as he kneeled to pick up a few branches.

Jared stopped chopping at a branch and looked at him. Then, he looked down at his hatchet and ran his thumb in a perpendicular direction across the blade as if checking for sharpness. He raised his eyes to the thick canopy above them, then looked at Josh.

"Cambria thinks you may still be alive in our world," he said.

Josh furrowed his brow, "What?"

"She thinks you may be in," Jared paused for a moment as if he were trying to find the right word. "Limbo. Perhaps you are barely hanging on in our world, yet present enough to be here. Maybe your pains are coming from there."

"So, do you think I am still alive?" Josh asked.

Jared shrugged his shoulders.

"I can't live in both worlds," Josh said.

"You might be, for the time being," Jared said.

"Who decides which way I go?" Josh asked.

Jared shrugged again and said, "Maybe the Great Fathers are pulling to have you in this world."

"And maybe God is pulling to keep me in my world."

"Maybe."

"Which one will win?" Josh asked.

"The side that needs you most."

#

They walked back to the pond, each with an armload of firewood. Jared carried more than Josh, but despite limping when they went to fetch the wood, Josh walked with only the slightest hobble. They dropped the dry branches in a pile near the fire.

Cambria walked the pond's edge, occasionally sprinkling something into the water. Tessa pulled marmalade and cheese sandwiches from a wicker basket and passed them to whoever wanted one. Dorn drove a wishbone branch into the ground on each side of the fire. He walked to one of the horses and pulled a burlap bundle from a saddle bag. He returned, laid it on the ground, and then pulled the burlap back to reveal a shiny, marbled piece of meat.

"What do we have here?" Jared asked.

"A gift," Dorn said. "A gift from a friend from the other side of the Snake River."

Jared narrowed his eyes and tilted his head slightly.

"I'll explain later."

"But what is it?" Jared asked.

"Mountain goat."

Dorn found a straight branch, stripped the bark, and wrapped the meat around it. He secured the meat with twine and set the branch onto the crotches of the twigs.

"This is for later," Dorn said as he adjusted the spit so it was centered over the flames.

While the sun hurled over their heads, Cambria continued to sprinkle different herbs into the pond, and she occasionally poured streams of water from the cup they had boiled earlier. The fire behind her sizzled as drips of fat fell into the flames. Sawyer entertained the party for a time, but soon enough, he was asleep on a blanket under the shade of the yew. Raistlin was the only other one asleep.

Late in the afternoon, Cambria walked to the campfire and said, "Okay, it's time."

Dorn took a deep breath and nodded to Cambria. Then, he looked at Jared as he approached the wagon. Jared followed, and they woke Raistlin from his slumber and slid him off the wagon. Raistlin swayed for a moment, but the other two men held onto his arms to keep him from falling. They walked him to the edge of the pond and helped him sit on the ground.

"What are we doing?" Raistlin asked in a weak voice.

"You have to go in the pond, Daddy," Cambria knelt and rubbed his back with one hand.

"Why?" Raistlin asked.

"It will make you better," she said.

Raistlin nodded, and his eyes were weary. He tried to stand and then sat back down.

"You have to take your clothes off, Daddy," Cambria said. "Down to your skivvies."

"Okay. Close your eyes," Raistlin said.

Cambria and Jared helped him out of his shirt. Then they pulled his moccasins off and tossed them aside. With a few tugs, he was out of his trousers. Jared and Dorn helped him to his feet.

Raistlin's body was pale and bony, and his skin sagged. His gray hair fell past his shoulders, and his beard was draped onto his upper chest. His underwear hung from his body, barely covering his privates.

They guided him to the edge of the pond. His toes touched the water. "You have to go from here, Daddy," Cambria said as she touched Raistlin's back. The others let go of his arms, Raistlin leaned forward, and his eyes rolled back for a moment. Then he stood up straight and looked out at the water.

"You have to walk in there, Daddy. We can't go any further."

The water in the pond was usually clear enough to see the bottom, but now it was milky white from the things Cambria had mixed in. The trees surrounding the pond reflected off the water.

Raistlin slowly waded, and soon it was over his underwear. The others silently watched as the fire behind them crackled under the cooking meat.

"How much more, Cammie?"

"Up to your chest, Daddy."

He walked deeper into the water until it was to his chest. He stopped, tilted his head back, and looked toward the tops of the trees.

"This is beautiful," Raistlin said. "The water feels wonderful. I am numb. And the sky looks like magic." Then he closed his eyes. "What now?"

"You have to lean back and fall beneath the water's surface," Cambria said. "Hold your breath for as long as possible until you fall asleep. You won't panic; medicine is in the water to make you feel comfortable. Just let it happen."

"Okay," he said. Raistlin leaned back and floated in the water. His toes poked above the surface. "Okay, Cammie. I love you."

Before Cambria could get out any words, Raistlin was below the surface.

They all lined the shore, anxiously waiting. Sawyer was awake in Tessa's arms. He looked around while he chewed on a finger. The others watched the ripples in the water disappear.

Dorn leaned and whispered in Cambria's ear, "What if this doesn't work?"

Cambria took her glance away from the pond and looked at the ground. Then she raised her gaze to Dorn, looked him in the eyes, and slowly shook her head with a frown. Then she looked back out at the milky pond. Tears welled in her eyes.

Minutes passed as they all watched over the pond. The birds in the trees chirped away, and squirrels and chipmunks carried on with their daily business as if nothing had changed.

The minutes that passed seemed like hours for those gathered along the shore. In the past, Raistlin had said, "Time is fickle." He may have repeated it if he had been one of those who stood on the shoreline that day.

The anticipation of Raistlin coming to the surface slowly faded as the long minutes passed. Each one of them had their way of expressing it. Josh dropped his head, turned, and slowly walked to the fire. Tessa began to weep. Nana took Sawyer from Tessa's arms and kissed him on the forehead. When Tessa dropped to her knees, Nan rubbed her shoulders with her free hand. Anastasia began to cry at the sight of her mother's distress. Dorn took a slow, deep breath and looked to the sky. Sally leaned her head on his shoulder, and tears streaked her cheeks. Jared clenched his jaw. The losses in his life had been too much; he couldn't comprehend another. Josh was now sitting in the grass a few feet from the fire. He was half dazed from the medicine but aware enough to understand the loss. Sawyer fussed at the boredom.

Usually, Dorn was the tough, stoic one; this time, it was Cambria. She stared at the middle of the pond where Raistlin had gone under. She didn't shed a tear. She seemed oblivious to the heartbreak happening around her.

When the bubbles began to appear on the pond's surface, Cambria was the only one who hadn't given up. The bubbles grew more prominent, and the sound attracted those who had turned away. They were all gathered at the shoreline again in a matter of moments. The milkiness of the pond began to dissipate where the turbulence was happening.

Then, the disruption began to calm; the large bubbles disappeared, and the small ones started to float to the surface. Raistlin's body floated to the surface in moments with his back to the sky. His pale skin seemed to glow in the late afternoon sun.

Something was different. The first noticeable change was the dark brown hair on his head instead of the gray locks he had before he went under. And his skin was tight to his body, not sagging like it was several minutes before.

He floated in the water with his arms spread wide. His dark brown hair floated around his head.

Everyone remained silent, all of them baffled at the scene before them.

Then Raistlin popped out of the water and flipped his long hair back, momentarily creating an arc of water above his head. He yelled triumphantly, raised his hands, and slammed them back onto the surface.

His hair was as long as it had been before he went under. The wrinkles in his face were gone, and he was trim and fit. He looked to be a man in his twenties. He waded through the waist-deep water toward the shore, where they all stood. Water drops dribbled off his now dark beard.

Raistlin smiled at the sight of his loved ones. He looked straight at Tessa and waded toward her. His privates began to show above the surface as the water grew shallow.

"Daddy!" Cambria yelled and then grabbed Anastasia, turning her away from the pond.

"Oh, silly me," Raistlin said as he covered himself below the abdomen. His voice was clear and thick. "I think I lost my underdrawers."

"I have clothes for you," Tessa said as the others turned away so Raistlin could leave the pond.

He beamed at his wife and mother of his children. He walked over to her, and they stood face-to-face. They were at eye level with each other because she stood on the higher part of the bank.

"Well, look at you," she said. "All young and strong." She ran her hand softly down the side of his face. Then she whispered, "I thought we were going to lose you." A tear ran down her cheek.

"Not a chance," he whispered back. He raised his hands from his privates and held each side of her face. "Great Fathers, I have missed this beautiful face." He pulled her face to his and kissed her. "It's been over thirty years. You have no idea how much I have missed you." Then they wrapped their arms around each other and shared a long, passionate kiss.

Once clothed, he yelled, "Okay, you can look now."

The others turned and cheered. Anatasia jumped up and down; her hair bounced on her shoulders. Although the man before her was much younger than her father had ever been in her life, she knew it was him. Cambria had told her what she did with the mouse and how it came out of the water much younger than when she had dropped it in the bowl. Cambria didn't exactly tell her that the mouse came back out as a baby, but she told her that her father would look younger when he came out of the water. Cambria didn't know how young he would be or if it would even work, but she felt her calculations were sufficient. This was the Raistlin she knew when she was growing up. The Fountain of Youth she created didn't make him too young; Raistlin Barrow had nothing but life before him.

Anatasia ran to him and threw her arms around his waist. "Daddy, I missed you!"

Raistlin leaned down and kissed her head, "I missed you too, baby."

Then Cambria walked to him. He smiled at her and said, "And I suppose you are responsible for all of this?" He held out his arms toward the pond.

She smiled and shrugged, "Guilty as charged."

He stepped forward, took her in his arms, and spun her around.

Once they finished their embrace, Nana stepped forward.

"Where the heck have you been?" She had a stern look on her face. "You young whippersnapper." Then the stern look turned into a smile, and she said, "Welcome home, Son."

Raistlin hugged his mother, and when he let go of her, he looked to his friend Dorn.

"Dorn," Raistlin said.

"Raistlin."

Raistlin touched his shoulder, "Thank you for coming to Detroit to find me. I would not have made it home without you."

"You would have done the same," Dorn said with a smile.

"Darn right, I would," Raistlin said, throwing his arms around his lifelong friend.

#

After all the greetings and things had settled down, they made their way to the fire. The meat on the spit was charred and dripping with fat. Nana sliced potatoes and seared them in a pan held over the flame. Then she threw sliced mushrooms and chopped onions into the mix.

Once the vegetables were cooked, Dorn began to slice pieces of the cooked meat above the fire and let the slices drop onto the thin stone slab, propped up with a makeshift stand made of small logs. Then, he portioned the meals into pottery bowls and handed them to his friends.

The afternoon was fantastic. Logs carved into seats years before surrounded the fire as they sat. They talked and laughed while they ate.

After Raistlin washed a bite down with some lemonade, he said, "Ah, Billy would have loved this. All of us together. Talking and having a great time."

Dorn stopped chewing and swallowed. Then he said, "I was going to wait to mention this, but I might as well bring it up now. Billy is alive."

All of them looked at Dorn. Those that were in the middle of chewing stopped. Anastasia's mouth fell open, and her eyes were wide.

"Is this true?" Tessa asked. "How do you know?"

"I believe it to be true," Dorn said.

"Where is he?" Jared asked.

"Lance has him," Dorn said. "He has him at the castle with…"

"All of the other children," Raistlin finished the sentence for him. "He has children from the town at his castle. He will not let them go home. I saw it all after the fight at the castle. It was as if I were having visions. The Great Fathers were there. They were telling me to go into caves that were behind me. That is when I saw it all. It was like I was there, but I could do nothing."

"When you told us this in Dee-troit and the In Between, I thought you were delirious. I didn't think it was true." Dorn looked down at his bowl momentarily, then back at Raistlin. "You were in and out of consciousness day after day; I thought maybe you were having hallucinations."

Raistlin nodded, "Understood."

Part IV: The Trek

Chapter 41

The three moons aligned a week after Raistlin walked out of Wendell Pond. He and Dorn leaned on a rock that was taller than they were.

"Are we ready?" Raistlin asked.

"Of course we are," Dorn responded.

They made their way through the pines and into the cave. When they entered, the three Great Fathers were already seated on their marble bench on the other side of the crystal clear stream.

Randall spoke first, "Well, I haven't seen you boys together since you were young lads."

Dominique nodded in agreement.

Asmund sat at the end of the bench with no response.

"To what do we have the pleasure?" Randall asked.

"We have some problems," Raistlin said as he sat on the Bubinga bench.

Dorn sat next to Raistlin and watched the three men across the stream.

"What types of problems?" Randall asked.

While Raistlin filled the trio in on the children who were held hostage at Erikson's Castle, Dorn watched the reactions of the three men. The Great Fathers knew everything that happened in Evergreen, so none of it was news to them. Their reactions were calm and understanding. As the conversation continued, they discussed Lance Erikson's evil ways. Asmund observed the conversation, never noticing that Dorn was paying attention to his reactions.

"If you choose to attack his castle to attempt a rescue of the children," Dominique said to Raistlin, "blood will spill." He leaned forward and glanced at Dorn, then back at Raistlin. "This would be an attack, what they would call an act of war in the other world. Expect him and his people to fight back. This can get ugly."

"There is too much at stake to do any different," Raistlin said.

In the past, Raistlin was the passive one. He was the one that never wanted to rattle the cage. Diplomacy was always the option for him. The quill was always mightier than the sword. Since he had learned more and more about Lance's actions, whether it was in some of his visions or from Teagan, he led the way toward an aggressive move against the castle on the other side of the river. Raistlin was convinced and as angry as a cobra trapped in a corner. He finally wanted to lead the way into battle, even though the battle had been Dorn's for decades.

"Lance is an evil person," Dominique said. "He is even more evil than his father was. Which I never thought was possible, but it is happening." The flame in the lantern nearest to Dominique flickered while he paused momentarily. "We haven't told you anything about the next world," Dominique held his hands towards Randall and Asmund and said, "The world the three of us live in." He dropped his hands and looked back at Raistlin and Dorn. "Lance Erikson is someone we do not need in that world."

"Is Ivan Erikson in your world?" Those were the first words Dorn had uttered since they entered the cave.

Dominique looked his son in the eyes, "Unfortunately, I cannot share that information with you."

Dorn nodded. He understood the rules. Nobody in Evergreen knew anything about the next world, and it would always stay that way.

"How do we keep Lance from moving on to the next world?" Raistlin asked.

"There is an arrow," Dominique said. "If one is killed with this arrow, their legacy stops there. At that point, it is all over. That person will not move on to any other world. Their existence in all forms ceases to exist."

As Dominique spoke of the arrow in more detail, Dorn glanced at Asmund. Asmund was engaged in what Dominique was saying. It was evident to Dorn that it was all news for Asmund.

"The arrow is unique." Dominique continued, "The fletching is from a Great Horned Owl, and it is touched with oil for a more sleek movement through the air. The shaft is made from Red Balau, and the arrowhead is made of quartz and zinc. Specks of gold are on the tip of the arrowhead." He shifted in his seat, crossed and uncrossed his legs. "Once you find it, you must make a prototype to practice with. It will fly differently than the arrows you are used to. This arrow can only be flown once. Whether it hits its target or not, the arrow will disappear once its initial flight is complete. It will reappear in the other world and could stay lost there for centuries." He paused briefly, then said, "It is referred to as the Crimson Arrow."

"Where can this arrow be found?" Raistlin asked.

"It is not in Evergreen."

"So, we need to go through another door?"

Dominique nodded.

"Where will the door be?" Raistlin asked.

It was quiet for a moment, then Randall said, "On the other side of Rickenback Mountain."

Dorn leaned forward, "Impossible! Nobody has ever crossed over that mountain and made it back."

"I know, Son," Dominique said. "But this is the only way."

Chapter 42

For the next few days, Raistlin, Dorn, and Jared made plans for a trek over Rickenback Mountain. They packed their packs, not knowing what they would encounter on the other side. Things like matches, tinder plugs, food for days, extra clothing in case it was colder on the other side, and a good, solid hemp rope were packed.

Even though everyone else at the Barrow Homestead knew about the trek they were about to take, the three left early one morning before the sun rose over the horizon so there wouldn't be a fuss over their departure.

They hiked a few miles until they stood at the base of the mountain. The three of them looked up at its majesty.

Rickenback Mountain held a special place in the hearts of those from Ironwood. There were many intriguing things about it. Those from Ironwood were buried at the base, and the top of the mountain towered far into the sky. If the cloud ceiling were low enough, the top of the mountain would jut into the puffy balls of cotton candy, much too far for a dragon to fly over.

As far as anyone could tell, the top of the mountain was the middle of a long ridge that went from north to south. The ridge held a razor's edge along its back. Plenty from Evergreen had hiked toward the top of the mountain, but any of those traversing over the razor's edge never returned. Eventually, everyone quit worrying about what was on the other side of the mountain.

Now, the three of them had to try to do what nobody had ever done: traverse over the mountain and make it back to tell about it.

For several hundred feet of elevation gain, the hike was easy. But after that, the terrain grew rougher and steeper. They all wore packs and used hiking sticks.

Once they broke through the treeline, there were no more distinct trails, unlike those at lower elevations. Raistlin, now being young and full of vigor, led the way. Dorn followed behind him. Jared kept falling further and further behind. The thin air they were dealing with at the high elevations began to take a toll on him, who was much more limited in lung capacity than his counterparts since his near mortal wound from Lance.

Once the terrain became so steep that they could barely move forward without doing some rock climbing, Jared hollered up to his friends, "I can't do it! I have to stop here." He held his chest where a sword had entered just months before. "I can't hardly breathe this high. The air is too thin." He put his hands on his knees and gasped for breath, then looked back up at them, "I'm going back."

Raistlin and Dorn looked down the slope at Jared. Raistlin acted as if the whole thing was a walk in the park. Dorn was winded, but not nearly as much as Jared.

Nothing was said between the three men. Only a trio of nods connected them before Raistlin and Dorn continued up the mountain, and Jared began walking back down.

Things grew tricky as Dorn and Raistlin ascended. They tried to navigate their way up the incline. There was no map to guide them. They were the first in generations to attempt climbing Rickenback Mountain. Sometimes, their navigation worked, and sometimes, it left them in a pinch.

During one instance, Raistlin had to shimmy his way across a small ledge. He leaned against the side of the mountain, his chest and belly pressed against the rocky terrain. The hemp rope was tied around his waist; the other end was tied to a tree trunk to Raistlin's left. One slip on the ledge would lead to sure death. The rope tied around the tree was a last resort in case of a fall. Once Raistlin was in a secure spot, he tied the rope's end around another tree. Then Dorn took the end of the rope and tied it around his waist, then shimmied his way over to Raistlin. They had to do this several times before the terrain became more forgiving.

The definition of a more forgiving terrain in this situation was a thin trail that hugged the side of the mountain; they could walk it, but they often used the steep slope beside them as a handhold. The trail zigzagged up the mountain. It was a natural trail, not one worn down by frequent hikers. The air grew thinner yet, and now both men were breathing heavily.

Soon, they were above the clouds that scattered like cotton balls below them, and the air was cold enough to see their breath. Ironwood could be seen as a small village nestled between the clouds. It was impossible to see anyone in the streets from this distance.

Instead of the razor's edge peak of the mountain towering over them, it was now just a few dozen feet away. The only problem was that there were no more flat surfaces to walk on, and the wall that stood before them had no handholds to help them reach the top.

They stood beside each other as they tried to catch their breath while looking up at the peak.

"What now?" Raistlin asked.

"Hand me that rope," Dorn said, not taking his eyes from the mountaintop.

Raistlin untied the rope from his side and handed it to Dorn.

Dorn walked back down the trail but still looked up as if searching for something at the top. Then he stopped, uncoiled a short amount of the rope, and held it in his other hand. He tossed the rest of the coil in the air. It uncoiled as it rose. The rope's end sailed over the top of the mountain but immediately snapped back and fell into a pile at his feet. Dorn coiled most of the rope and tried again. This time, the rope didn't even make it over the top.

He was aiming for a crease in the rises of the peak. One rise was shifted slightly to the side of the other. Dorn thought that if he could land the rope between the two, it might wedge in the crease. Hopefully, it would be enough to stay in place to use as a climbing rope. He quickly stopped paying attention to how often he tried to land the rope on its target, but before he knew it, the rope held.

He tugged on it, and it grew taut. He looked at Raistlin and smiled. Raistlin pulled his glance down from the top and smiled back. Raistlin's dark hair and his young, fit frame made Dorn feel like they were in their twenties again.

"You ready?" Dorn asked.

Raistlin nodded and said, "Let's hope that The Great Fathers are watching over us."

Dorn pulled on the rope and put his feet up against the vertical mountainside; then, he began climbing to the top. Once he reached the top, he swung one leg over the ridge to help hold himself up and looked to the other side. The terrain on the other side wasn't nearly as steep, but it wasn't level enough to walk on for several dozen feet below. He pulled his entire body over the ridge and lay on the other side at an angle just steep enough that he wouldn't slide down the terrain.

"Come on up," he hollered down at Raistlin.

Raistlin didn't hesitate. After a few minutes, he was lying on his belly on the other slope next to Dorn. He pulled the rope up and tossed it over his shoulder. The wedge at the ridge still held onto the rope. They both had to tug on the rope to loosen it.

Raistlin coiled the rope and hung it from his side. Both of them rolled over and looked down at the valley.

A river curved back and forth from the base of the mountain. Trees hugged the riverbanks, surrounding a vast body of water into which the river emptied. The surrounding lands were rolling plains. On one curve of the river, a village wrapped itself around the outside of the bend. The village looked empty. No smoke came from the chimneys; nobody walked about the dirt streets that meandered around various dwellings with no particular pattern or order of the street layout. The fields outside the village waved at them with their tall, wild grass. From their vantage point, no crops were on any open plains.

The body of water in the distance kept pulling at Dorn's attention. "Look at all that water," he said. "And how blue it is."

Raistlin looked at the water and said, "I have read that is what the ocean looks like."

"Incredible," Dorn whispered.

"Let's go," Raistlin said as he began to scoot on his behind down the slope.

Eventually, the terrain leveled out enough for them to hike again. The walk down was rocky. Only the smallest spruce trees poked out of cracks in the rock. As they descended, weeds became more prominent around the large stones, and the air grew thicker and slightly warmer.

They had to resort to their trusty hemp rope when they reached a ledge that dropped too far to jump. They looked for another way, but the only option was to go over the edge. Dorn tied the rope around a rock and tossed it over the ledge. He held his hand out in a gesture for Raistlin to go first. Raistlin obliged and descended. When Raistlin finished with the rope, Dorn pulled some of it up and lay the slack on the ground. He overlapped the rope three times and then made a set of loops. He tucked the ends of the overlaps into the loops and pulled the rope tight. He leaned back to be sure the knot would hold his weight. The loops at each end held the overlaps and made three parallel ropes between them.

143

It looked like a primitive three-stringed instrument. He pulled his dagger and cut the rope in the middle. The knots held. He descended, and in seconds, he was standing next to Dorn. He shook the rope several times, hard enough that the rope slapped against the wall. The knot at the top broke free, and the rope fell to them. The section tied around the rock, which Dorn had cut with his knife, remained at the top of the small cliff —a fair tradeoff for a safe descent.

They continued down the mountain until dark grew near. They still had several hundred feet to go until they reached the bottom but decided to camp for the evening.

They lit a fire and warmed rocks while sipping tea and tugging on salted goat meat. Once the fire died down, they slipped the warmed rocks into the bottom of their sleeping sacks. It was a technique Jared had taught them. Then they slipped into their sacks and stared at the stars for a time before they both fell into a slumber.

After a small fire and a cup of tea in the morning, they stuffed their packs and finished the last descent down the mountain. Their shadows grew shorter as the sun rose higher in the sky. By the time the burning ball was directly over their heads, they had reached the edge of the village.

The dwellings were smaller than those on the Barrow Homestead and in all of Evergreen. The doorways were short enough for Raistlin and Dorn to duck to get through. Had Billy Blaine been there, he would have experienced a wave of awesomeness after feeling so tall in such a small dwelling. The dwellings were also skinnier, with steeper roofs and taller, thinner openings that acted as windows.

Dorn and Raistlin began to walk through the village. Once they realized it was indeed abandoned, they separated and investigated the dwellings separately.

The hinges on the doors stuck for a moment, then protested as the doors were opened. Inside the dwellings, short logs stood on the dirt floors; they must have worked as seats for the primitive folk. A few houses had a stone fireplace with a short chimney barely passing the roofline. There was no rhyme or reason to the layout of the little houses; besides the log stools, there were no shelves or counters; the buildings were simply shelters for eating and sleeping. A few of the dwellings had skeletons lying on beds of feathers. Some skeletons were still clothed in buckskin or wolf pelts. The skeletons were as short as children. There was no food in sight. Primitive utensils, such as clay cups, wooden spoons, and stone knives, were scattered about. Once seen up close, it was apparent that many of the buildings were on the verge of crumbling.

Outside the dwellings, log stools were scattered in some areas. Small wood piles had been reduced to miniature logs and sawdust. Stone axes stuck into some of the trees; the tree bark had grown around the heads of the axes.

It was evident that this primitive village hadn't shown signs of life for decades, maybe even centuries. Had Dorn or Raistlin's great, great grandfathers come over Rickenback Mountain and found this village, it likely would have been in the same state as it was now.

They met back out in the dusty street.

"What happened here?" Dorn asked.

"I can't believe this has been here, just across the mountain, and we didn't know about it," Raistlin said.

"That's not your typical mountain we crossed. Although, you'd think we would have traversed it in the past." Dorn said.

"The Great Fathers always told me it wasn't worth the risk," Raistlin said. "They said there was fertile farmland, but moving multiple families over the mountain was impossible. My father and I always thought it would be a waste of time."

"So, what did happen here?"

Raistlin shrugged his shoulders, "Who knows? It seems difficult to believe they starved." He nodded toward the fields beyond the town. "You could grow anything out there."

"Why are they such small people?"

"On Earth, there was a smaller version of humans in their prehistoric era," Raistlin pulled a piece of goat meat from his vest, tore it in half, and handed a piece to Dorn. "Maybe this was their afterworld."

They stood silently for a few moments, taking in the empty town.

"What now?" Dorn asked.

"The ocean?"

"Sounds good," Dorn replied.

They walked toward the edge of town. The roads began to straighten, and the houses grew further apart. Then, they walked down a lonely road with trees on one side and open fields on the other. Birds chirped at each other in the treetops, dozens of them arguing about this and that. One bird swooped down on the road before them. It was a small white bird with black on the top of its head. It hopped back and forth in front of them. Both men stopped walking when it was apparent that the bird was not going to get out of their way.

"Wait," Raistlin said. "That is my grandfather's favorite bird. It's a black-capped chickadee."

The little bird gave a soft sound every few seconds, just two notes that melted in with all the other bird songs. After a few more bounces, the chickadee flew in a circle above their heads. Then, it flew further, landed, and bounced back and forth across the road. This repeated as the men walked in the direction of the bird. Just as they approached their feathered friend, the bird flew off again and landed ahead of them. After several attempts to fly forward and bounce around the road, the bird took flight to its left into the trees. Dorn and Raistlin watched it go and continued in the same direction they had been traveling. The bird flew out of the trees and circled over their heads several times. It dropped to the ground, stood before them, and looked at them. The men stopped, looking at the bird. Then, the bird retook flight and flew into the trees.

"Maybe it's trying to tell us something," Dorn said as he watched the bird go.

"Maybe," Raistlin said. "Let's follow it."

The chickadee led them through the trees, zipping back and forth over their heads, singing its song. They followed.

Soon, they could see the river flowing its way to the ocean. The bird changed direction, and they walked with the river to their left.

Dorn held out his hand across Raistlin's chest to stop him. "Hey," he said. "Look." He pointed.

A tree larger than all the rest caught their attention. It was the largest tree trunk they had seen since they crossed the mountain. At the base of the tree, a door stood. It was a short door, just a bit shorter than the ones in town. It was a wooden door with brass hardware and an arched top.

"That's where we have to go," Raistlin said.

They stopped before the door. The base of the tree was flat on the front, where the door stood, and the rest of it had bark all the way around. Raistlin looked at Dorn and nodded, then he pulled the door open.

#

This time, the In Between was uneventful. There were no blizzards or deserts to challenge their way. There were no polar bears or prehistoric birds to threaten their lives. It was just a trail through a group of trees. The sky was a bit dreary, and foilage fell from the branches. Hues of yellow, red, pink, salmon, and orange landed softly on the ground. The air was still and calm. It was like the perfect autumn day.

They walked for a time; the trail meandered left and right.

"Seems awful nice compared to the last time we dealt with the In Between," Dorn said as he glanced at the treetops.

"I don't think Lance's gods knew we were going over the mountain this time," Raistlin responded.

"Surprising," Dorn said.

"What do you mean?"

"I just didn't have a good feeling when we met with the Great Fathers," Dorn said.

Raistlin stopped walking and turned, which caused Dorn to stop. "What are you talking about?" Raistlin said.

"Something strange is happening."

"I am still not sure what you mean."

"I don't trust what I see and hear in that cave."

Raistlin furrowed his brow, "Dorn, your father meets in that cave."

"It's not him."

"My grandfather meets us there. He is almost your grandfather, too. He watched you every step of the way while you and I grew up."

"I know," Dorn said while he nodded, "and I would trust him with my life."

The wind began to stir, sending the colorful leaves into a swirl. Thunder rumbled in the sky.

"Asmund?" Raistlin asked. "Is it him?"

Dorn looked off to the side with no answer.

Raistlin shifted on his feet. "Asmund Edmund was one of the greatest pioneers of Evergreen. Ironwood wouldn't exist without him."

Dorn stayed quiet for a moment, gazing off into the distance.

"How can you not trust him?" Raistlin asked. "He has always looked out for us."

Dorn sighed and said, "I don't like his body language. He also acts like some of the info my father and Randall shared is news to him. You have to watch his movements closely when the others are talking."

Rain began to fall, and thunder rumbled louder. Lightning streaked across the sky as the drops passed through the leaves and branches.

"They must know we are talking about them," Raistlin said as he began walking again.

Both men were soaked by the time they reached another door. The door was similar to the one they had walked through hours earlier. There was a burlap bag that hung from the door handle. Raistlin grabbed the bag and started pulling things from it. Everything inside the bag was dry. First was a driver's license.

Raistlin looked at it and said, "It looks like my first name is Mason again."

Cash and a credit card were in the bag, along with a key fob for a car. He tossed the burlap bag aside and pulled the door handle.

Chapter 43

They stood on a city sidewalk. Although it wasn't pouring rain like it was on the other side of the door, the smell of autumn filled the air. They both jumped at the honk of a car horn. Raistlin had lived in Detroit for three decades, but the city life seemed odd to him even though he had only been back in Evergreen for a short time. For most in the city, the horn was an everyday occurrence. Once they realized the horn wasn't directed at them, the men began to walk down the sidewalk.

They came to a corner, and Dorn began to walk into the street. Raistlin tugged on Dorn's shirt sleeve and pulled him back. "We have to wait," Raistlin said.

Once the crosswalk signal turned green, they walked across the intersection. They could see a river and the banks on the other side through some of the gaps between the buildings. Dorn stopped walking and pulled a book from his vest. It was the Book of Secrets.

Raistlin stopped and watched as Dorn opened the book to a random page. A pencil drawing of an arrow lay diagonally across the page. Both men knew that it represented the special arrow they were looking for.

"So, it's telling us we must find the arrow," Raistlin said. "We already know that; that is why we came here."

"Wait," Dorn said. "Look."

Dorn had the book in a horizontal position. He rotated the book, but the arrow continued to point in the same direction, toward a point near the river. A moment ago, the arrow was diagonally draped across the page. Now, it sat horizontally on the page. Dorn rotated the book another ninety degrees, and then the arrow was pointed toward the bottom of the page.

"It's pointing to where we need to go," Raistlin said.

They took a right at the next intersection and walked down the sidewalk toward the river. Dorn held the book before him, occasionally rotating it. The arrow held its place like a needle on a compass.

Minutes later, they stood on a sidewalk and looked across at the other river bank. Short black posts connected with large black chain links separated them from the water. The buildings behind them created shadows that stretched almost to the other side of the river.

"The arrow must be over there on the other side, somewhere," Raislin said. "It will be dark soon. We should find a place to stay, and we can walk across that bridge in the morning." He pointed momentarily to the smaller two bridges off to their left.

#

They found a hotel in the heart of downtown and checked into their room. The room had two beds, a recliner, an office chair at a small desk, a refrigerator, and a bathroom. When Dorn went to the window and pulled the curtains aside, they had a great view of the river and the bridges that crossed it.

"This Toledo town seems much smaller than Dee-troit," Dorn said as he looked out the window. In moments, the sun would completely disappear below the horizon.

"Much smaller," Raistlin said.

They ate at a fancy bar on the top floor of the hotel. It was much too fancy for their liking. They were used to wooden bar stools and a floor that creaked when someone walked into the saloon in Ironwood. This bar featured tall, padded chairs, a carpeted floor, and vibrant furniture. Dorn wasn't used to having so many choices of whiskey.

"Just give me the one with the eagle on the bottle," he finally told the girl who was waiting on them.

Raislin chose the chicken marsala, and Dorn picked the lemongrass skirt steak. By the time they finished their first drink, the meals were brought to the table. The chicken dish was smothered with gravy and mushrooms. Mashed potatoes and a small heap of vegetables were beside the chicken. The steak dish had asparagus on the side. Once again, they admired the food of the other world. Seasonings were incorporated into this food and hadn't been discovered in Evergreen yet. They enjoyed a few more drinks and gazed at the city lights for a while. Dorn was still getting used to Raistlin looking so young. In the past, Dorn was always the one that looked younger. Raistlin's hair turned gray much sooner than one would think, so Dorn's dark hair gave him an edge in the aging department. Since the fountain of youth, Raistlin's hair had been dark, as it was when he was in his twenties. His crow's feet had disappeared, and he was fit. Dorn's stubble showed signs of gray. The roles had reversed.

They ate breakfast in the hotel the following morning, a buffet near the lobby. The choices at the buffet were vast: scrambled eggs, a waffle griddle, fruit, biscuits and gravy, hashbrowns, red potatoes, white or wheat toast, jellies and jams, bagels, muffins, and various puddings for dessert. A chef was stationed at a flat-top grill to make omelets to anyone's liking. Raistlin had a three-egg omelet with sausage, green peppers, and onions sliced and diced inside. Dorn had three biscuits drowned in sausage gravy with scrambled eggs on the side. They both had apple juice to drink. They ate like pigs, and soon, they were on their way.

The arrow still held steady on the page as they walked down the sidewalk. The morning air was damp as they walked between tall buildings. The sun lit the intersection ahead as its rays barrelled onto the street through the big gap between two mini skyscrapers. Once they reached the crossroads, they turned right and walked toward the sun, which warmed them on the cool morning.

They walked across a small drawbridge and saw three other bridges from their vantage point. The most impressive one was to their left. Piers shaped like elongated octagons held the roadway over the muddy river. The main pier poked hundreds of feet into the sky, and large cables stretched out to help hold the roadway below. Two local refineries and a nuclear power plant in the distance put off steam that drifted straight up into the sky in the still air.

Every few minutes, Dorn checked the book; the arrow pointed straight ahead. On the other side of the river, construction was being done on the riverbanks. It appeared that a riverwalk was being constructed. Off to the right was a row of restaurants with patios at the back, which met a sidewalk that ran along the water. To their left was another restaurant, followed by some housing lofts. They continued to walk straight at the next intersection, waited at the crosswalk for the green walk light, then headed across the street. The street signs at the intersection indicated that it was located at the intersection of Main and Front. From here, the road took them up a slight hill. They passed a few shops, a few bars, a tobacco shop, and a liquor store. There was less hustle and bustle on this side of the river. There were no tall buildings or parking garages. It looked like the main attraction on this side was the restaurants.

As they made their way up the low incline of the hill, the arrow started to drift to the left. Just slightly at first, but as they neared the next intersection, the arrow moved more and more. Once they reached the intersection, the arrow was pointing directly to their left. They changed direction and crossed the street. Now, they were on a street called Starr. The arrow was pointing straight ahead since they had turned. They passed a few streets on the left; then, they passed a bar and a convenience store. There was a gas station across the street and then a pawn shop on the other side. Once they passed the pawn shop, Dorn opened the book again. This time, the arrow was pointing behind them and to the left. Dorn stopped and took a few steps back. The arrow started to drift forward, and when he stood directly in front of the pawn shop, it pointed to its front doors.

A bell that hung from the door rang as they opened it, and it rang again when the door swept itself shut. Inside the shop, glass cases and countertops made a "U" shape around the shop. In the glass cases were wristwatches, pocket watches, jewelry, coins, cell phones, baseball cards, electronic devices, video game consoles, pocket knives, hand crafted pens, candle holders, whiskey flasks, small pottery dishes, fancy cutlery, leather wallets; it would've taken several hours to see everything inside the cases. Behind the cases were guitars, banjos, golf clubs, baseball bats, coo-coo clocks, and framed paintings hung on the walls. There were also several shelves on the walls with baseball mitts, brand-new baseballs, sleeves of golf balls, small picture frames, whiskey decanters, rocks, glasses, wine stoppers, bookshelf speakers, books, knives in leather sheaths, and pottery. The store was crowded and disheveled.

In the corner to the right of the entrance, a compound bow hung on the wall with a quiver of arrows hanging next to it. Dorn and Raistlin spotted the bow simultaneously and walked up to the counter, where the items were displayed. The shopkeeper handed cash to a lady who had just pawned an item. She turned toward the door, stuffing the money into her blouse. The bell rang as she left.

The shopkeeper looked at Dorn and Raistlin, nodded, and said, "How you gents doing today?" He was a man of medium build. He wore a cowboy hat and had a toothpick sticking out of the corner of his mouth.

"Can I see that quiver of arrows?" Raislin asked politely.

"Sure thing." The man walked over, pulled the quiver off its hanging hook, and handed it to Raistlin.

Raistlin pulled one of the arrows from the molded plastic contraption. The tip was three shiny razor blades that met to form a point like a small pyramid. The fletching on the other end was made of soft brown plastic. The shaft was covered in a camouflage pattern, which Raistlin thought was silly. Good luck finding a camo arrow in the brush if you missed your target, he thought. He shook his head and put the arrow back. He tilted the quiver to see the tips of the other arrows. None of them were the arrow that Dominique had described to them. None of them had a tip speckled with gold or a shaft made of Balau. He handed the quiver back to the shopkeeper.

"Anything in particular you're hankerin' for?" The man asked, then he pointed to the bow. "You wanna see the bow?"

Raistlin shook his head. "We were looking for an arrow." He glanced at some of the other things on the wall. "A special arrow."

"That so?"

"We were told you would have it here," Raistlin said.

The man leaned forward over the counter, "I don't sell stolen goods, mister."

"I didn't say it was stolen."

"Then what you sayin'?"

"He's saying you either have the arrow here or you had it here before," Dorn said as he leaned forward to engage in a stare-off with the shopkeeper.

The shopkeeper shifted his toothpick from one side of his mouth to the other as they eyed each other up. "What's this arrow look like?"

"It has a shaft made of Balau and has a quartz tip speckled with gold," Raistlin said.

"What the hell is Balau?" the man asked and then waved the question away. "I sold it earlier today," the man said. "Got a pretty penny for it, too."

"Who bought it?" Dorn asked.

"That, my friend, is my business," the man grinned.

Dorn grabbed the man's shirt and pulled, "It's our business!"

The man pulled a handgun from his belt and held it inches from Dorn's head, "Wrong!"

"Whoa!" Raistlin held his hands up and took a step back.

In a quick movement, Dorn grabbed the man's wrist and slammed it to the counter. The man yelled in pain as the gun slid off the counter and clanked on the floor at Dorn's feet.

"Great Fathers!" Raistlin said, quickly going to the door and turning the lock. He tugged on the door to ensure it was secured.

Chapter 44

They sat in the shop's back room. A bag of ice was draped over the shopkeeper's wrist. He worked a mouse with his other hand and clicked through pages on a computer screen.

"What's so special about this arrow, anyway?" The shopkeeper asked as he slid video clips from left to right across the screen.

"You have no idea," Raistlin said. "I couldn't explain if I tried; you wouldn't understand." He sat on a folding chair and leaned toward the small screen for a better look.

"Is it money? Because I charged them a small fortune."

Raistlin glanced at the man and said, "It's got nothing to do with money."

The man shook his head, pulled his hand from the mouse to shift his toothpick, and said, "I kinda wish I would've sold it to you two. I didn't like the fella with the black hair. The girl he was with was pretty, but I didn't trust her either; money is money, right?"

Dorn glanced from the screen for a second to look at the man and said, "I guess so."

"Here we are," the man said and clicked on one of the video clips. It was from a camera high up on a wall at the rear of the showroom. The front door was in the center of the video. The bright light from outside made the store seem dim and dusty. A man and a woman walked through the door and glanced around. The glare outside made it tough to make out any features of the two that had walked in; they were just silhouettes. After taking a good look around, they walked to one side of the store and examined the items in the glass cases and on the walls.

The shopkeeper clicked his mouse, and the camera angle changed. Now, it was a camera on the side of the showroom. Raistlin, having seen similar footage from his shop when he lived in Detroit, was impressed by the video's quality.

It was obvious to Raislin and Dorn who the people in the video were. Lance had his hair pulled back in a ponytail, and his earrings sparkled for a moment with the turn of his head in the right light. Brenna stood next to him; her blonde hair fell over her shoulders. They both wore leather vests; Brenna had a white blouse under hers, and Lance was bare-skinned, showing off his tattoos. There was no sound, but Lance spoke to the shopkeeper in the video. He smiled and nodded during the exchange while Brenna watched. She would glance at Lance briefly, then across the counter at the shopkeeper. Her eyes were calm and easy as they glanced back and forth. They shifted to their left as they looked at things in the cases, Lance and the shopkeeper talking the entire time. Then, the shopkeeper pointed across the showroom. Lance and Brenna looked over their shoulders and went to the other side.

He clicked the mouse again, and they looked at another angle. As the shopkeeper pointed and spoke, Lance and Brenna looked into a glass case. Soon, Lance had the Crimson Arrow in his hand. Money was handed across the table without bickering, and Lance and Brenna left the shop.

"How long ago was this?" Raistlin asked.

The shopkeeper pulled the ice from his wrist and looked at it. "Yesterday," he said without looking up.

Raistlin grimaced. "Did they say anything that gave you a clue where they would go?"

The shopkeeper put the ice back on his wrist, looked up at Raistlin, and shook his head.

Chapter 45

After they had a quick drink at the sports bar two doors down from the pawn shop, Raistlin said, "I have an idea." He slid a few dollars onto the bar, nodded at the bartender, and headed out the door. Dorn followed.

"Where are we going?" Dorn asked.

"Back across the river," Raistlin said. "Every downtown has a library."

"What about that gadget you got out of the burlap bag? Didn't the vehicle we used in Detroit have one of those?"

Raistlin stopped walking and reached into his pocket. He pulled out the key fob, looked at the symbols on the buttons, and pushed the one with the horn. "Listen for a horn," he said. He pushed the button again, but they couldn't hear it.

They continued to walk down Main Street and over the bridge to the other side of the river. They took a left on Summit Street. Raistlin pushed the horn button on the key fob every few hundred feet. This reminded Dorn to check the book, but the pages were blank.

Raistlin politely stopped a young woman walking in their direction and asked if there was a library in town. He quickly explained that he and his friend were staying in town for a few days for a relative's wedding.

"There sure is," she said and pointed in the direction she came from. Her hair was in dreadlocks, and bracelets hung from her wrist. "Go to Adams and take a right. Go up a few blocks; the library is on Adams and Michigan."

"Thank you so much, ma'am," Raistlin said.

The woman grinned at him for a moment and said, "No problem." Then she hesitated for a second and said, "Sir!" She smiled at him again and said, "Enjoy your stay; I hope the wedding is beautiful." Then she turned and went on her way.

They reached the library a few minutes later. While they stood on the sidewalk and gazed at the building, Raistlin pushed the button on the fob again. This time, they heard a horn. They looked at each other, and Raistlin did it again. Dorn leaned his head to the side and pointed at an angle toward the ground.

"It's coming from down there," he said. There was a curved drive that went down below the building. They walked down the drive and found a parking area under the building.

Raistlin pushed the button again; a car's lights flashed, and its horn sounded. They walked to the car. It was a gray mid-sized sedan. Raistlin opened the driver's side door and looked inside.

"Where are we going to go?" Dorn asked.

Raistlin shrugged his shoulders. "I don't know," he said. "We may not have to go anywhere."

"If the Great Fathers wanted us to have a vehicle when we came here, wouldn't that mean we should be going somewhere?"

"You have a point," Raistlin said as he shut the car door. Then he pointed toward the doors that led to the library's bottom floor.

They walked into the building, and a hallway led them in various directions. They took a stairway to the main floor. The building opened up in a sense of modern architecture that Raistlin hadn't seen during his time in this other world. Although books surrounded them, the openness of the atrium made them feel like they were in an observatory rather than a library.

Raistlin approached the desk. A pretty woman in a blue blouse greeted him with a smile.

"Hello. I am looking for some information that would have been in a newspaper. Probably the Detroit Press," Raistlin said.

"Well," the woman said. "All of our microfilm is a little prehistoric," she giggled. "Most of the recent stuff, you could do an internet search on one of our computers over there."

Raistlin gave a half smile and said, "I'm not sure how to do that."

The woman smiled and said, "I'll help you." Then she led them to one of the computers. "What are you looking for?" she looked up at Raistlin after she asked the question. Her palms were braced on the keyboard, ready to type.

Raistlin sighed for a moment and thought. He crossed his arms and said, "Someone I know was involved in an accident in Detroit, but I haven't heard anything beyond that."

"Okay, when did it happen?"

Raistlin rubbed his forehead with one hand, "August of 2022."

"So," she said. "We are only talking a few weeks ago if that. Do you have a specific date?"

Raistlin shook his head, "I'm not sure of the exact date."

"That's fine," she said as she began typing. "What's the person's name?"

"Josh Collins."

She clicked away at the keys while Raistlin and Dorn watched as the computer screen changed. "Yep, there's one," she said. "It looks as though there have been a few stories about this over the past ten days or so." She showed Raistlin what tabs to click with the mouse to read each article and left them alone.

Raistlin glanced over the first article and then summed it up so Dorn wouldn't have to read over his shoulder. "Josh Collins was injured in a hit and run and is at Henry Ford Hospital in critical condition," Raistlin said. He silently glanced over a few sentences and said, "Witnesses say it was a bus that struck Mr. Collins.

Local authorities are still searching for the bus and the driver." Raistlin clicked the next tab; the article's title read "Wolves Spotted in the Collins Hit and Run." Raistlin began to read again, "Reports have emerged that wolves were spotted at the hit-and-run scene. Two witnesses have spoken on the incident, saying that they drove by the scene moments before Collins was struck by a bus, and two wolves were fighting with a big dog. The only wolves that exist in Michigan are in the Upper Peninsula. It is very rare for a wolf to be seen in the southern part of the state. Mr. Collins remains in a coma at Henry Ford Hospital."

"How long ago did it happen?" Dorn asked.

Raistlin pointed to the date in the lower right corner of the computer monitor and then looked at the date of the first article. "Ten days ago," he said.

"So we were here ten days ago?" Dorn asked.

Raistlin looked at him and nodded, "I know it seems odd. Time is different between the two worlds." He looked at the monitor and said, "We have to go to Henry Ford Hospital."

Chapter 46

With a map they printed at the library, Raistlin drove the car out of the parking garage, and they made their way out of town. Raistlin was cautious as he went; he didn't drive much while living in Detroit. They took Interstate 280 to Interstate 75 and headed north. In minutes, they crossed the state line and were driving in Michigan. The roads went from smooth to rough once they passed the "Welcome to Michigan" sign.

The scenery was trees, cornfields, power plants, refineries, and the occasional body of water. Dorn took it in for a time, then asked, "What was it like living in this world for thirty years?"

Raistlin didn't take his eyes off the road, and his hands gripped the steering wheel while he drove. "It was humbling."

Dorn glanced out his window, "What do you mean?"

"I missed Tessa. I missed Cambria and Anatasia. I missed you. It was a lonely time. Incredibly lonely. Every morning I woke, I felt that was the day I would return to Evergreen. Every single day! For thirty years." He stretched his fingers out, then regripped the wheel. "Then you, Jared, and Billy brought me back." He momentarily took his eyes off the road and looked at Dorn, "I'll never forget that."

In typical Dorn fashion, he didn't respond to the statements. They rode silently for a few minutes, then Raistlin said, "But it also reminded me of what we have to do."

"Go on," Dorn said.

"We have to take over Greystone. We have to free those children."

"My, how the tables have turned," Dorn said as he smiled at Raistlin.

"Okay, I'll admit it," Raistlin said. "You were right all along. We have been at war with Lance the entire time. Now it is time to do something about it."

#

They made their way into the heart of Detroit; Dorn read the directions they had printed. Soon, they were parked at Henry Ford Hospital. They made their way to the main lobby, and Raistlin went to the front desk to ask for information on Josh's location. The man at the desk gave him directions to the proper ICU ward but told Raistlin that he wouldn't be allowed into the room since he wasn't family.

"So, we won't see Josh?" Dorn asked while they rode in the elevator.

"We can figure out a way," Raistlin said as he looked above the elevator door to follow what floors they were passing.

They got off the elevator and looked around. It was a small waiting room that went around the corner, so the room was in the shape of an 'L.' Not far from the elevator doors, a man sat in his chair, holding a hardcover book before him. Around the corner, three people sat quietly chatting. They passed around a bag of popcorn.

Raistlin and Dorn approached a desk, but the only thing there was an empty chair and a note. "Out to lunch. Return: 1 pm." The sound of the ICU doors opening turned Dorn's attention. A young woman walked through the double doors, which closed as soon as she passed through them. It was Samira. She wore sandals, cut-off jeans, and an oversized white top. Her hair was disheveled, and her eyes were darkened by pain. She looked at Dorn for a moment, looked away, then looked back with widened eyes.

"Dorn!" she said and hurried toward him. Even though they hadn't even carried on a conversation a few weeks before, when Samira jogged toward Dorn, there was evidently a bond. She hugged him and said, "What are you doing here? You left! You all went through the arch!"

"How is Josh?" Dorn asked.

"He... I..." she scrambled for words. "Why are you here?" She looked beyond Dorn where Raistlin was.

"That's Raistlin," Dorn said.

She gave a confused look. "What?" she said.

Dorn glanced over his shoulder and then back at her, "It's him."

"Who? Who's Raistlin?" She said.

Raistlin stepped forward and smiled. It was the shyest he had been since the fountain of youth. "Hi, Samira. It's Mason; your friends lived next door to me and watched my dog, Atticus."

Samira took a step back, "Mason, who?" Then she gasped, held both hands to her mouth, looked at Raistlin, and back at Dorn.

"It's him," Dorn said.

"How?"

"There was a fountain of youth. It's hard to explain."

Samira put her hands to her head and pulled on her hair. "None of this makes sense," she said. "I thought Josh was crazy, and now you are telling me the old man with the nice dog that lived next to my friends stumbled across a fountain that made him look decades younger?" She stepped back a few steps. "And all of this was your fault." She pointed a thumb over her shoulder, "The love of my life wouldn't be in this ICU if you two hadn't shown up."

Raistlin stepped forward, "They came to rescue me. What started all of this happened before you were born. It's me, Samira. Mason. Well, Raistlin." He held out his arms.

"I must be going crazy," she mumbled. Then, she hugged Raistlin.

She stepped back, ran her hands through her hair, and said, "Josh. You asked about Josh."

"How is he?" Raistlin asked.

Samira looked at them through eyes that had endured days of tears. She closed her eyes and dropped her head, "His parents are with him now; we are deciding what to do." She held her hand to her mouth. "He is fading." She looked up at them, and her eyes welled with tears. "They amputated his leg, but he hasn't gotten out of his coma due to a head injury. His brain function is fading. He was good for a time, but he is just fading. He called for me, for Jared, but now he is silent." She dropped her hands to her sides and looked at the two men, "I think we are going to have to let him go." Then she crumpled to the ground and bawled.

Dorn and Raistlin both draped over her and let her cry.

Raistlin put his hand under her chin when she settled down and raised her head, "Tell them to hang on."

"What?" she asked as she looked at him.

"Tell them to wait," Raistlin said, pulling her to her feet. "We may be able to save him."

"What?" She said again. "How?"

"Let's grab some coffee," Raistlin said as he held out his arm. She tucked her arm in his elbow, and the three of them headed toward the elevator.

# #

Raistlin carried three coffees to a table where Samira and Dorn sat. They were tucked away in the corner of a cafeteria.

"Josh is in Evergreen," Raistlin said.

"Oh, my God!" She said. "This is crazy! This is ridiculous! This is crazy!"

"He got there before we did," Dorn said. "We had quite a journey to get back. When we got there, he was already at the homestead."

"How can he be in both places?" She asked.

"He was in great pain when we first arrived," Dorn said. "Cambria was caring for him. He was in and out of consciousness for several days."

Samira sat motionless.

"Soon, he was on his feet, and the pain lessened to a point where he didn't need medicating," Raistlin said. Then, he took both of Samira's hands in his. "Cambria thinks he is floating between the two worlds, and it hasn't been decided which way he will go. I think he is fading here in your world because he is getting stronger in Evergreen."

Samira closed her eyes and sighed.

"If Dorn and I return to Evergreen in time, we can turn things back around with Cambria's help."

Dorn pulled the book from his vest and opened it, then looked at Raistlin, "The Riverwalk."

Raistlin nodded and looked at Samira, "We have to go."

She walked them to the lobby. "Will I ever see you guys again?"

Raistlin glanced at the ground and then looked her in the eyes. He shrugged, "I don't know. I guess it depends on what your God has in store for you."

"Well," tears started to roll down her cheeks, "I hope my God sends me to Evergreen."

Raistlin pulled her in for a hug and whispered in her ear, "Maybe the Great Fathers can help with that."

"I hope so," she whispered and hugged him back. "Please be careful," she whispered in his ear.

Raistlin said, "Of course."

Dorn politely put his hands out to embrace hers, but she pushed them away and threw her arms around his neck for a hug. She held on to him and said, "Weeks ago, I would have thought all this other world stuff was just sci-fi, but Josh was determined to convince me it was all true. When I met all of you, it was amazing." She pulled back from the hug, put her hands on his arms, and looked into his dark eyes. "I know I have many years left in this crappy world, and I want to spend them with Josh. Please, do whatever you can to make that happen."

Dorn nodded, "You have my word." Then he reached into his vest and pulled out the Book of Secrets. "Here," he said as he handed the book to Samira. "Jared wanted Josh to have this back. It was a book he bought when he was a kid. I don't think we will need it anymore."

Samira took the book and said, "I will give it to him."

#

Once they reached the car, Dorn said, "You know how to get to the Riverwalk?"

Raistlin looked at him as he pushed the button that started the engine, "I spent thirty years here, remember?"

Dorn nodded, "That is all still really hard to comprehend."

They exited the parking area, got on Trumbull, and headed for the river. Once they were through Corktown, they took a left and headed for Lafayette Park. They took a turn to the right and parked in the lot at the Riverwalk. It was the same lot where, just days before, they fought with Lance and Brenna, and Josh was hit by the bus.

They saw the arch before they got out of the car.

Chapter 47

Once they were back in Evergreen, Raistlin asked Cambria, "How has Josh been?" They were down at the barn, checking the slumber sand cache.

"He's getting better and better," she said as she jotted a note down on a piece of parchment. "His leg hardly bothers him, and he seems to be sleeping uninterrupted."

Raistlin remained quiet for a moment.

"What is it, Daddy?"

"We saw Samira when we went looking for the arrow," Raistlin said.

"Okay," she dropped the parchment and pencil to her side.

"Josh is fading in his world. Fast." He brushed his hair back. "They are thinking of letting him go."

"Oh, no," she whispered.

"I think you were right. I think he has been in a state of limbo between our world and his. All the pain, yelling Samira's name and Jared's name in his sleep. Now things are better here, but worse there." Raistlin backed out of the cache closet, and Cambria followed; then, he put the padlock on the latch and locked it with a click.

"That does make sense," Cambria said, then looked at Raistlin. "We have to tell Jared. Josh has to go back. I wasn't sure before, but it has to be true; he is drifting between two worlds."

#

"What do you have to do?" Jared asked her.

"We have to tell Josh first," she said as she touched Jared's arm. "We have to convince him that he has to go back."

"We can convince him. There is no doubt, but then what do we do?"

"I have to do some reading. This is more than slumber sand. I have to find a concoction that will work." Her beautiful brown eyes found his. "There is just no way to test it." She placed her hands on his chest. "But, first, I have to show you something."

#

"This is the biggest secret in Evergreen," Cambria said.

Raistlin put the key in the padlock and turned it. He pulled it off the latch and slipped it into his vest. He opened the door, and some shelves held little vials of slumber sand.

"I've been here," Jared said. "You know that."

Cambria shook her head and walked into the cache. The small room was just tall enough that Raistlin didn't have to duck when he entered after her. It was narrow enough that they couldn't go around one another once they entered. Jared and Dorn followed them in. Dorn pulled the door shut. Raistlin struck a sulfur match and lit a lantern on one of the shelves. The flame jumped for a second, then he adjusted the knob, and it settled to a warm glow. Cambria walked through the narrow storage space to the far wall. It also had shelves, but they were full of odds and ends like empty jars, lids, spoons of different sizes for measuring, another lantern, and screens for filtering minerals like sand and crushed roots. She grabbed one of the shelves and tugged at it. The entire wall shifted. It turned like a lazy susan that was too old and rusted up to move more than an inch. She tugged again, and it moved a bit more. The pivot point was in the center of the wall. One side of the wall was moving toward them; the other was moving away. She kept tugging while the others watched. Soon, the wall stood perpendicular to where it had moments before. Cambria grabbed the other lantern off the wall and held it toward Raistlin. He lit another match, and the lantern was glowing a second later. She slid through the small opening, and the rest of them followed.

They stood in a small space, barely large enough for the four of them to fit. The other three walls were wood planks. They were darkened with age and absorbed much of the light from the two lamps. Cambria set the lamp on the floor and kneeled. She felt her hands around and pried a wooden latch from the floorboards. She pulled on the latch, and a portion of the floor came up with it. Dorn reached down and helped her pull it to the side. A ladder led down into darkness. She stepped down onto the first rung and began to lower herself. She grabbed the lantern and continued down. Once she was at the bottom of the ladder, a glow could be seen around her. The others followed as Dorn waited at the top of the ladder to go down last.

Once they were all at the base of the ladder, the glow of both lanterns revealed what was in the room.

On all four sides were shelves of books. Some of them were thick, and some were thin. Most were bound and covered with dust.

"What the hell is this?" Jared asked.

"These are the books I have learned from," Cambria said.

"Where did they come from?" Jared asked.

"Some were found in various places in Evergreen," Raistlin said. "Some were found in your world. Once we sensed that Cambria had something special as a child, the Great Fathers told me and my father the secrets of where to find them."

"It's Evergreen's best kept secret. Does anyone else know about this?" Jared asked.

"My father, Nana, and Tessa know, and Dorn, of course," Raistlin said.

"How have you kept it such a secret?"

Raistlin shrugged.

"Mylo didn't even know?" Jared asked. "As much time as he spent in this barn."

"Had he ever found the secret wall, he never would have fit through the space."

Jared raised his eyebrows for a moment, "Yeah, I guess that's true."

Cambria moved toward one of the walls of books. The moving lantern made it look as though the spines of the books were slowly moving across the shelves. "There are ideas between these covers, potions, recipes; some are in different languages."

"You can read these different languages," Jared asked.

Cambria nodded.

"Why didn't I know that until now?"

"Being multilingual doesn't mean much in Evergreen," she said. She looked at him without a smile and then turned to the shelves. She read the spines on the books and began to pull a book here and there. She handed the books to Raistlin and Jared. She glanced over the spines on the other walls, pulling a few more books. After she went around the room, she looked at them and said, "Okay, let's go."

They passed the books up the ladder and then passed them through the secret door, and Dorn stacked them on one of the shelves in the cache.

\#

Jared and Cambria fell behind Raistlin and Dorn as they walked up the hill to the cabin, all of them carrying books.

"How will this go?" Jared asked.

"If I can figure it out correctly, it will be like putting your dog down, but much slower," Cambria said, glancing over at Jared. A lock of curly hair blew across her face.

"Will it be peaceful," Jared asked.

"Yes, I wouldn't do it if it wasn't."

Chapter 48

The cabin was quiet as the sun fell to the horizon that day. As Sawyer went about the deck, Tessa sat on the wooden furniture with Raistlin. Inside, Cambria loomed over the pages in front of her. She took notes on several pieces of parchment, and when she closed the book and set it aside, she grabbed another and started to look through it. Dorn sat on a wooden chair across the table from her. He traded glances from watching Sawyer out the window to Cambria studying the books before her. He remembered when Cambria was as young as Sawyer. He had watched her grow and always stood by her side as a friend. He never scolded her; he felt that was Raistlin's job. He taught her how to hunt and how to fight. He made knives for her and taught her how to throw them. Eventually, Dorn had the great blacksmith of Evergreen, Abraham Polk, make her a set of knives that fit her hand perfectly and were balanced better than any knife she had ever held. He grinned at the memories while he sipped whiskey from a glass.

Now and then, Cambria would say the name of a root or a stone, and Dorn would jot it down on his parchment. After flipping through several books, Cambria looked at him and nodded at Dorn's glass. Dorn reached up on the shelf, grabbed a glass and the bottle, and poured a whiskey for her.

Jared and Josh sat on their beds, facing each other. They spoke quietly. At times, their foreheads would touch, and they would hold hands while they cried. Jared explained what had to happen. Josh agreed. They wondered aloud if they would ever see each other again, and they both decided to fight like hell to make it happen. Eventually, they crawled into their own beds and faced each other, sometimes reaching out to hold the other's hand. They fell asleep, not remembering the last exchange between them that night.

While they slept, Raistlin and Tessa slept in their room with the baby. Nana snoozed away in her room. Cambria continued to give Dorn a list of items she would need in the morning. Dorn added to his list, occasionally refilling his glass and tossing a log into the stove.

Although Dorn was the last to fall asleep that night, he was the first to rise in the morning. He was out the door before anyone else woke. He had a burlap sack slung over his shoulder, his sword hung from one side of his belt, and a hatchet from the other. He quickly trekked through the countryside and harvested various roots from the ground. He went to the river and found some of the rocks Cambria needed. The rocks made a barrage of percussion sounds as he dropped them into the sack; some clinked against other rocks, and others knocked against the roots. He kneeled and scanned the bank to see if there were any that he missed. Once he was satisfied and began to stand up straight, he heard a horse snort behind him. He turned, thinking it was Raistlin and America, his trusty steed.

It was not one horse but two. Raistlin was not riding either one of them. Lance was atop one of the horses, Brenna on the other.

"Well, well, well," Lance said as his horse rode closer to the riverbank. "Mr. Hale! What are you doing? Splashing on the riverbank?"

Dorn stood straight and spun the burlap sack to keep the top closed. He stepped toward Lance, but Lance held up his hand.

"Hold on, my friend," Lance said. "How long has it been? The last time I saw you was on the banks of the Detroit River. What was that? Two? Three weeks ago?"

Just as Dorn was about to speak, Lance interrupted him, "And speaking of Detroit, how can you still bow to your," he put his hands in the air, made quotation signs with his fingers, and said, "Great Fathers" then dropped his hands and continued. "After they left Raistlin in that city for three decades?" He tilted his head back, laughed, and said, "Do you call him Daddy now since he is so old?" Then Lance held his hand to his mouth and said, "Oh, shoot, there I go again. I always slip up and bring up your daddy."

"I'll say it again," Dorn said in a cool tone. "I am going to kill you. Probably not today, but I will kill you. I am going to spill your blood for all to see. Your daddy's shadow isn't here anymore either; he is dead. I will spill your blood on his grave."

Lance's eyes squinted at Dorn in evident scorn.

Shunk!

Dorn and Lance looked toward the source of the sound. Brenna backed her horse a few steps. A knife was stuck in the tree just a few inches from where her face was moments before.

Cambria approached, walking with her fists at her sides and a grim look on her face. Her curly hair flowed behind her shoulders. Brenna pulled her bow and began to nock an arrow, but Cambria pulled another knife from her vest and threw it. It flew end over end and struck Brenna's arrow, breaking it into splinters.

Dorn dropped the burlap sack, pulled his sword, and flashed it in front of the face of Lance's horse. It spooked the animal, and it rose, standing on its hind legs. Dorn pushed his sword under the horse's chin as it stood tall. The horse could not drop back down onto its front feet; Dorn put more pressure on its throat with his sword every time it tried. The horse tried to stand taller to get away from the sword, which caused Lance to fall off the horse. Dorn immediately backed away, and the horse trotted to the river bank. Lance leaped to his feet and pulled his sword.

As Brenna reached for another arrow, Cambria pulled two more knives from her vest. She could have had both knives in the air before Brenna had the arrow in her hand. Brenna realized the predicament and grasped the pommel before her. She scowled at Cambria. The two kept their eyes on each other while Dorn and Lance squared off.

Lance attacked Dorn's torso with a jab of the sword. Dorn blocked it and took a defensive stance, anticipating another attack. Before Lance launched another attack, hoof steps were heard. In an instant and a cloud of dust, Raistlin rode atop America and raced between the two men. Dorn and Lance stepped back and watched as the horse spun around and faced them. Raistlin pulled on the reins, and America rose, and then the horse dropped back on all fours. America looked young and sleek. Raistlin pulled his sword and pointed it at Lance. Lance looked at him as if he was seeing a ghost. Raistlin was an old man the last time he had seen him, several days before, in Detroit. Now, he was looking at the Raistlin from decades earlier.

"Get out of Ironwood," Raistlin said, still pointing the sword at Lance. "Don't ever come back. We've been through this. You are NOT welcome here!"

Lance was so flabbergasted by Raistlin's appearance that he was speechless for the first time in his life. He put a better grip on his sword and looked at the horse. America pinned his ears back, scraped the dirt with one hoof, stood up on his hind legs, threw his nose toward the sky, and neighed. When America was back on all fours, he glared at Lance, his ears still pinned back.

It was an outnumbered situation for Lance and Brenna. There was nothing they could do but walk away from the confrontation. Five of the best fighters in all of Evergreen were gathered under a massive oak on the banks of the Snake River, and the faceoff would result in a stalemate.

Lance gathered in the situation and walked to his horse. Cambria backed away from Brenna's horse and let her pass. Dorn and Raistlin watched her go by. Once Lance was atop his horse, he nodded at Brenna, and they trotted down the riverbank toward the bridge. After they traveled several dozen yards, Lance turned his horse.

"Raistlin Barrow," he held one hand to his mouth to help project his voice as he yelled. "I have the Crimson Arrow! One of you will not make it to the next world. I will be sure the shot is true!" Then he turned his horse back around, and they disappeared around the river's bend.

They watched them go, and then Raistlin turned to Dorn and Cambria and said, "You both okay?"

Dorn nodded. "It was nothing. They snuck up on us," he said, then nodded toward Cambria. "but she saved the day." Then he turned to her, "How did you know?"

She shrugged, "I didn't. I wanted to take a walk before I had to take care of the things that will happen today." She looked toward the river and squinted her eyes for a moment. "I hate that woman!"

"Anyone that would have relations with Lance Erikson is evil," Raistlin said.

Dorn walked to America and began to rub his snout. In return, America started to sniff Dorn's vest. It was common for Dorn to have a carrot or two in his vest in case he stumbled across one of his favorite horses or dragons. Today, there were none in his vest. America snorted in disappointment.

Dorn grinned, ran his hand down America's neck, and admired his shiny fur.

"What did you do to him?" Dorn asked.

Raistlin smiled, "I had him wade through Wendell Pond."

Chapter 49

It was a day of goodbyes, mourning, and rejoicing. It was the day they had to say farewell to Josh. If Cambria's plan were to work, he would leave Evergreen and return to his own world.

"It's just how it has to be," Jared told her through tears the evening before. "Mom and Dad need him. He has a future. It was different for me. He needs to be there." Then he looked at Cambria and said, "And I need to be here."

"You do," she kissed him on the forehead. "You do."

Jake flew in on Brutus after reading a note that Raistlin had sent with a dove.

The day started with a big breakfast. After the meal, they walked and rode horses to the base of Rickenback Mountain, where they walked among the grave markers. Josh kneeled before Billy's marker and pulled a few weeds that had grown around it.

"Josh," Jared said.

"Hmm," Josh tilted his head slightly toward Jared.

"We plan to attack Lance's Castle to get him and a bunch of other children that are being held hostage."

"I want to help," Josh said.

"You have to go home, Brother. I can take it from here."

#

The day continued with laughter and love, and although it was not the Day of the Feast, it was a feast nonetheless with a small group. Josh grew ever so dreary as the sun set. He winced in pain quite often, and when he stood, he favored one leg and walked with a limp. They had a campfire, and Raistlin broke out the harmonica and played sad songs. Cambria made one last concoction, and Josh drank it while sitting by the fire.

Finally, Josh stood, and instead of bidding them goodbye one at a time, he spoke to them as a group. "I want to thank you for everything you have done for Billy, my brother, and me. I hope I find my way back here someday. I love every one of you." His voice broke with the last words, and he quickly turned away to head toward the cabin. However, the quick movement threw him off balance. Jared promptly reached for him and saved him from falling. Jared put his arm around Josh's waist and walked him through the cabin door and into the bedroom.

Josh was delirious as Jared tucked him in. He pulled the blanket to his brother's chin as Josh shivered in the cool room.

"Do you want me to close the window," Jared whispered.

"No," Josh mumbled. "I want the fresh air."

"Okay," Jared whispered, turning to pull a curtain away to let in the moonlight.

"I love you, Jare," Josh mumbled.

"I love you, too," Jared said, turning back from the window, but Josh was already snoring. Then he leaned down and whispered in his ear, "Tell Mom and Dad I love them."

Jared crawled into bed and tilted his head on his pillow to watch the stars while he listened to his brother breathe. He lay there for an hour as the stars shifted their positions beyond the trees. At times, Josh mumbled the names of his mom and dad, Jared, Samira, and even Billy.

Jared woke to the bed next to him creaking and blankets flapping. The moonlight was no longer a square on the floor; it had climbed up the wall. It was just light enough in the room that he could see his brother's arms flailing under the blankets. He hurried to the oil lamp on the table by the bedroom door. Josh was mumbling words, but louder than earlier.

"Jare! Jare!"

"I'm right here, Brother!" Jared scrambled to light the lamp.

Josh said his brother's name two more times.

Jared lit the lamp and adjusted the flame. The room lit up. The blanket on the bed that had covered Josh bubbled up for a moment in the air, then it drifted back down onto the bed and settled as if someone had tossed it to try to cover someone up. The blanket lay flat on the bed. Josh was gone.

A small commotion was heard at the other end of the cabin, and footsteps padded down the hall. Jared stood and looked at the blanket his brother had slept under moments before. First, Raistlin came to the door wearing his nightshirt. He glanced at the bed and closed his eyes for a moment. A second later, Cambria stood next to him. Raistlin nodded to Jared, kissed Cambria on the forehead, and walked away from the door. Cambria came through the door and threw her arms around Jared.

Jared's sobs were what woke the rest of the cabin. They lit a candle and sat around the kitchen table. Talking was little and far between. Jared joined them with red eyes and no words. The only sounds were the creaking of Jake's rocking chair and the occasional sip of tea.

Once the light on the morning horizon began to show, Jared asked Cambria, "Do you think he lived?" He paused for a moment. "I mean, in my world. Do you think he made it?"

Cambria had been leaning her head on his chest for over an hour. She looked up at him and said, "Yes. Yes, I believe he did."

Dorn and Sally were the only ones to get a whole night's sleep since they stayed in their own cabin every night. When Dorn walked into Raistlin's cabin shortly after the sun rose, he saw the somber looks on their faces. He stopped and nodded. He turned to the door and then turned back to the group and said, "I'll start a campfire. Sally and I will cook breakfast outside." He looked at Jared and gave him a quick nod while the corners of his mouth tugged downward for a moment. Jared nodded back.

Tessa and Nana helped Sally with the biscuit mix while Dorn popped back inside and had Anastasia come with him to gather eggs and salted bacon. They also picked blueberries and strawberries on the way back.

It was a great breakfast and the start of a new day. The sun warmed them, and soon they were all smiling.

Jared would always wonder if his brother was okay.

Part V: Preparations

Chapter 50

Ten days after being struck by a bus, Josh Collins woke from his coma. Samira had been sleeping in the chair next to his hospital bed. She woke with the sounds of his mumbles. He was saying his brother's name and her's and Billy's. She held his hand while his consciousness slowly appeared. The nurses came in and checked on him while he woke.

Samira met with Mason, whose name was Raistlin, depending on which world he was in, and Dorn only a few days prior. They said they would go back to Evergreen and try to save Josh for her. Now, he was waking up in her world.

The nurses kept him busy after he woke. They asked him questions and ran a few quick tests. Then they left so he could rest.

"Welcome back," Samira said and kissed his hand.

"Why am I in a hospital?" Josh asked in a weak voice. "Why am I in a hospital?"

"Josh," she said. "You were hit by a bus. Do you remember?"

He shook his head.

"It was down at the Riverwalk. Your friends were here."

"I was just in Evergreen," Josh said.

"I know."

He glanced over at her, "How do you know?"

"Raistlin and Dorn came here two days ago to check on you," she leaned forward to get closer to him. "But Raistlin was much younger."

Josh closed his eyes and said, "Cambria made a fountain of youth. She's good with things like that. She was the one that got me back here." The last of his words drifted off, and he began to snore.

#

Josh spent ten more days in the hospital and began outpatient physical therapy upon release. His leg had been amputated due to the accident, and he was fitted with a prosthetic leg. He missed the following semester of college but returned to classes after that. Samira dropped out of her dentistry degree and pursued a degree in Business Administration.

On the anniversary of his accident, Josh and Samira were married in a small ceremony in his Uncle Joe's barn. Atticus, the Airedale Terrier, stood next to them as they said their vows. Family and close friends were in attendance, and a DJ played tunes well into the evening.

The day of their wedding was also the anniversary of Attticus's injury. As he and Billy ran toward a scrum near an archway at the Riverwalk, Atticus realized his master was a part of the chaos. The hair on his back pointed up in anger, and he tugged on the leash. Billy tried to hold onto the leash with both hands, but Atticus broke free anyway. Two people in the scrum became wolves and met him in the attack.

As a stray dog in his younger years, he had been in a few scrapes or scuffles with other dogs. These interactions were usually over a scrap of food, not life or death. This time was the real deal. He was fighting not only for himself but for his master. There would be no cowering away or giving up. He fought the best he could, but the wolves were big and fast, and the injuries piled up quickly. They bit and tore at him; tufts of hair and clumps of skin were pulled from his body. One massive bite broke his shoulder. The wolves had a peculiar scent about them; it was the smell of a plant that he couldn't place.

Suddenly, the wolves ran off, and his master was gone. The arch was no longer there either. As Atticus lay on the ground, he heard Samira screaming. He lifted his head and saw her on the sidewalk, leaning over Josh, who lay in a heap on the ground. A bus sped off in the distance.

Once Atticus was out of the animal hospital, he stayed with Samira's roommates while Samira tended to Josh, first at the hospital and then back in Hickory with his parents. Atticus looked pitiful in his cast, and much of his body was shaved due to the need for his cuts to be stitched up. He reveled in the attention he got from Samira's roommates.

Once Josh returned to Detroit to continue his studies, he and Samira got an apartment together, and they moved Atticus in with them.

Atticus lived beyond his years. He had a long life for a dog of his breed, but it all had to come to an end one day. He began to have trouble getting around, his accidents in the house became more frequent, and his appetite was dwindling to nothing.

Josh knew the signs. One Saturday morning, they took him to the vet for what would be his last time. As Atticus was drifting off from his shot, Josh kissed him on the forehead and whispered in his ear, "Run to Evergreen. You will like it there. Tell my brother I said hi."

The words circled in his head as he drifted off to sleep.

#

Atticus felt that he had only slept for a moment and was back on his feet. He tried to lick Josh's face, but it was like he missed. Josh didn't pay any attention; he only wiped away tears. Samira sat beside Josh with her face in her hands. Her shoulders went up and down as she sobbed. Atticus looked down to see what Josh was focused on. A dog lay on the table. Atticus was confused at first, but when a small spot of light on the wall caught his attention, it all started to make sense. The small spot on the wall grew bigger. Soon, the spot grew to a hole in the entire wall. The hole was a tunnel, and at the end of the tunnel was a light.

Atticus jumped off the table and walked to the tunnel. He turned and looked back at Josh and Samira, who were mourning over him on the table. He gave a quick bark at them. Samira raised her head; she didn't look at him, but she did look in his direction. Josh smiled as he continued to look at the dog on the table.

Atticus turned and ran into the tunnel, never looking back at his old world. His aches and pains disappeared as he ran, and he felt young again. Not young like a pup, but young enough to be full-grown with boundless energy. His stride grew longer as he raced through the tunnel. He was running toward the light at the end, which became more significant as he went. His excitement rose as he drew closer to the end. He began to bark as he ran.

Minutes later, he burst out of the tunnel into bright sunshine. He skidded to a stop to take in this new world. He turned around and saw the tunnel he had just come from. Suddenly, the tunnel vanished, and a rock wall appeared. Atticus looked up, and the wall went as high as he could see. He sat with the rock wall at his back and looked around. To his left was grassy, rocky terrain that slowly led up a mountain. To his right was the back side of a castle. He took in the scene to decide what to do next. The smell in the air was familiar; it initially sent a shiver of fear through his veins, but then anger and a desire for revenge took over. The smell was of a plant, and he recognized it this time. The plant was called patchouli. It was the same scent he smelled on the wolves that had put him in the hospital. He realized he was in the same world from which the wolves came.

Chapter 51

As the weeks went by, Billy began to trust Teagan more and more. The day that convinced Billy to have faith in him was when Teagan slipped him a piece of jerky while Billy worked in the kitchen. At first, Billy thought nothing of it. He knew Teagan had been longing for his friendship, which Billy was fine with, but when he took a tug of the jerky, he immediately knew it was from the saloon in Ironwood. The hickory smoke flavor with a touch of pepper and orange zest gave it away. Even when he lived on Earth, he had never tasted beef jerky as good as this. This jerky had the smokiness that demanded the flannel shirts of autumn, but the zest took him to the beach on Lake Huron. When he tasted the jerky after Teagan handed it to him, he looked up, but Teagan was walking out the kitchen door and up to the main level.

This exchange convinced Billy that he and Teagan were on the same side. Not only had Teagan been telling him information that only Dorn or Raistlin would know, but the jerky straight from the saloon was icing on the cake. He knew Teagan was on his side, and Billy was ready to do whatever he asked.

Billy was smart enough to realize that Lance had a bigger plan; he had a vision. Many of the children his age worked in the kitchen, the stables, the garden, or the slaughterhouse; many jobs were needed. But there were also children of other ages there. The children in their later teens went on hunting expeditions and were taught the ways of the sword. These children were kept under lock and key. They weren't allowed to associate with the other children, and they ate and slept in separate quarters from the others.

One day, after Billy was relieved of his duties, he snooped around the castle. He found the sleeping quarters of the other children. He found an unlocked door and entered. The room housed many beds and their own little cafeteria. A wide, concrete stairway went up at the room's far end. At the top of the stairway was a set of metal doors. Billy knew these doors led to the outside. The same doors sat at ground level on the castle's north side. He quietly walked up the steps and tried the doors. They were heavy but moved the slightest bit. They were impossible to open from the inside as he knew they would be because the doors were always chained on the outside.

He found his way back out of the quarters by the way he came in. He wandered around the castle. He passed a guard now and then. The guards didn't bother any of the children who walked in permitted spaces, but if one was caught somewhere they shouldn't be, then punishment was in order. The hallways on the castle's first floor were lit with wall sconces. The sconces lit the stone walls and floor, and their light was barely bright enough to light the wooden rafters several dozen feet above. Various doors led to rooms on the left and the right. Some were living quarters for the castle's residents. Most guards, cooks, and helpers lived in quarters on the edge of the castle property. Only the elite lived in the castle. Most lived on the main floor, but Lance and his choice friends lived in the upper parts of the towers.

Billy kept snooping around the hallway, poking his head in open doorways. He took the first set of stairs he encountered. They spun their way up along the outer wall. There was a tall, skinny window every time he got to the east side of the stairwell. The view out the windows at first showed the curtain wall, but once he was at a higher elevation, he could see the houses on the outskirts of Greystone. When he rounded the final section, a guard stood in front of a door at the top. The guard shook his head. Billy immediately turned and went back down the stairs.

He continued through the hallways. At the base of one of the stairwells, a guard stood. Billy knew that those stairs led to Lance's quarters. Only a select few were allowed to pass by the guard and ascend the stairs. Billy kept moving through the hallway. He found another stairwell, which didn't have a guard at the bottom. He climbed the circular stairs, and when the stairway went around the third time, there was a window. Billy looked out and saw a portion of one of the lower roofs. Men were building some contraptions using large sections of wood and thick ropes. He watched them work for a moment, then continued up the stairs. At the top of the stairs, a guard slept under another window. Billy ignored the window and snuck to the top step. The guard snored lightly. Billy tried to open the door the guard was supposed to protect, but it was locked. Billy didn't know if the guard was supposed to keep people out of the room or keep someone inside. Before Billy ascended the stairs, he looked out the window. Now, the working men were below him, and their project seemed much bigger from this vantage point. It was hard for Billy to figure out precisely what they were building, but much of the wood was made of long, thin logs. Billy was spooked by the guard snorting in his sleep, so he quietly descended the stairs.

Chapter 52

Just days after Josh left Evergreen, the three moons aligned. Raistlin and Dorn sat on the large rocks amongst the pines.

"What do you plan to ask them?" Dorn said as he looked at the stars.

"What we should do now, and how did Lance know about the Crimson Arrow," Raistlin said.

Soon, they lit a lamp, passed through the trees, and walked into the cave. The other side of the cave was dark, so they couldn't see much past the stream. Raistlin adjusted the wick on his lantern, and the flame grew. The glow made its way to the other side of the cave.

When Raistlin registered the scene in his brain, he whispered, "Jesus wept." It was something he had never said while in Evergreen and was a testament to his efforts to find some faith during his three decades in the other world. Once he saw two of the Great Fathers dead on the other side of the stream, he suddenly wondered if the Great Fathers were the wrong diety to be following most of his life. While in the real world, he often thought of wearing a cross around his neck, but he never donned one. Now, he wished he had one around his neck to hold in his hand.

Dorn gasped at the scene before them.

Randall Barrow sat on the bench, leaning against the wall behind him. His dead eyes stared at the roof of the cave. His throat was slit, and blood covered the front of his white robe.

Another figure lay in a heap on the ground. It was evident that a struggle had happened. Raistlin held the light down low to get a better look at the face resting on the stone floor. Dorn's father was dead on the ground; part of his head was bashed in. Dried blood stained the floor around his upper body. Both bodies looked blue and cold. This atrocity had happened some time ago, and the culprit could be anywhere by now.

Dorn yelled a fierce yell, ran to the stream, and tried to jump across to the other side. Raistlin reached out and grabbed him, trying to pull him back. Dorn almost fell into the stream, but only his foot was immersed in the water before Raisltin took him to the floor. Dorn wrestled with him, and they rolled around, grunting and swearing. Dorn freed himself and stood. If he had crossed the stream to the other side, his life in Evergreen would have been over. It is the easiest way to "cross over" to the other side, but nobody knew the consequences of doing so. It was a form of suicide. Would one exist in the other world by doing this? Or would it all end? Would taking the easy way out end that person's journey forever? Nobody knew.

"I told you I didn't trust Asmund Edmund!" Dorn yelled. Raistlin was kneeling on the floor, catching his breath. "I told you!"

"I know you did," Raistlin said in between breaths. "Now, I believe you."

Dorn put his hands on his knees and started to weep. Not only was his father murdered in this world, but he was also murdered in the next. For Dorn, there were no more Great Fathers. Had his father not been one, it would have all seemed like smoke and mirrors. He doubted them after Raistlin's ordeal in Detroit and their difficulties getting through the In Between while bringing Raistlin back home. Raistlin blamed it on "Lance's Gods," but Dorn was always skeptical. He trusted his father more than anyone, including Randall Barrow, but he never trusted Asmund Edmund. It disappointed him that his father and Randall hadn't seen through Asmund before it was too late. It disappointed him more that he wouldn't see his father in the next world. Maybe he would see him in the world after that? He didn't know. He had no idea if there was anything more after the next world. If Dorn became an all-seeing Great Father when he reached the next world, he would ensure the ship was tight. Nobody would double-cross the people he would be protecting. He didn't know who would be the next Great Fathers. It might be three that he had never met, similar to Asmund. It could be someone who lived in Evergreen generations before Dorn.

He kept his hands on his knees, and his breathing slowed to normal. Raistlin stood and hugged him, "I am sorry, my friend. I didn't know." Then he whispered in Dorn's ear, "Let's go home. We'll make a plan and free the children, and then we will destroy Erikson's Castle."

Chapter 53

The next day, Raistlin, Dorn, and Jared spent the afternoon moving large boulders into the mouth of the cave. They stacked and stuffed them into the entrance. Then, they moved small fallen trees and branches and filled gaps or crevices. They showered the outside of their work with dirt and leaves.

Wherever the next Great Fathers would meet them remained to be seen. One day, they would discover where that place was. Perhaps one of the dragons would lead them there. Raistlin first found his way to the Great Fathers through a dream in his early twenties. In the dream, he was told about three prophets who would aid him in his life's decisions, and he had to embark on a journey to find them. Although the location of the cave wasn't far from the homestead, it took him several days to find it.

After the first day of the trek, he sat by a campfire and chewed on salted goat. He wasn't sure where he planned to go the next day. As he watched the flame lean slightly in the breeze, he noticed the smoke blowing in the opposite direction. The smoke was blowing into the breeze. It was the oddest thing in the world, but he knew it was a sign. He tried to see where the smoke was going, but the light from the fire prevented him from seeing into the distance. He waited while the logs burned and the flames shrunk. When the logs were embers, the smoke continued to roll off the glow and drift into the breeze. At this point, he could see landmarks where the smoke was going.

The following morning, he headed in the direction that the smoke had been drifting the evening before. He followed to the best of his memory, and when he felt he had reached where the smoke had been heading, he camped for the afternoon. When dusk came, he lit another fire. Once again, the smoke drifted in its direction, which had nothing to do with the direction of the breeze. The following day, he hiked until he felt he had arrived at the location where the smoke wanted him to be. He did this for five nights, sometimes covering only a few hundred yards a day, camping while the sun was still high in the sky.

The evening he found the cave, the smoke drifted straight into a group of pines to Raistlin's right. He pulled one of the logs from the fire and used it as a torch. The smoke led him to the mouth of a cave. This was the cave where Raistlin would meet with the Great Fathers for years.

Now, it was covered with camouflage. It would be centuries before someone would discover the cave again.

Chapter 54

Lance leaned against the pillows that rested on the headboard. Brenna rested her head on his shoulder. Her blonde hair was loose and spread over her chest. The sheets were pulled up to Lance's waist. His pale chest had a tuft of black hair. He smiled as he looked at the arrow in his hands.

"We have the Crimson Arrow," he said.

"Yes, we do," Brenna said, looking up at him. "Now what?"

"We have one shot, then it disappears."

She put her arm across his chest and rested her chin on her forearm, "So, who are you aiming for?"

"Who do you think?"

"Hmm," she stared at him, mesmerized by his good looks.

"Dorn Hale," Lance said, holding the arrow before him with the tip pointed toward the ceiling.

"I understand your history with Dorn," Brenna said. "But there is nobody else you would want to stop from going to the next world?"

"Of course not," Lance pulled his gaze from the arrow and looked at her. "Who do you think the arrow should kill?"

"Cambria Barrow."

Lance furrowed his brow, "Cambria?"

"Of course," Brenna said. "It's the only one that makes sense."

"Elaborate, my dear."

"Hit Dorn where it hurts, he and Raistlin both." She ran her fingers down one side of his face with a gentle touch. "Cambria is like the daughter that Dorn never had, and I am sure it wouldn't hurt you if you put a dagger in Raistlin's heart by killing his daughter." She smiled at him and said, "It is the only plan that makes the most sense."

One side of Lance's mouth pulled to a smile, "You, my dear, are a genius."

Chapter 55

"I've had visits with the townspeople," Teagan said. "They know you plan to release the children from Erikson's Castle. Many have stepped forward to volunteer." They were sitting in a dark corner of the saloon. Teagan wore his hat low to keep any light off his face. Dorn, Raistlin, and Jared sat around the table, listening to him. "If we get too many people involved on my side of the river, we take a chance of the wrong people finding out."

"Agreed," Raistlin said. "We should include as few as possible. How much does Billy know?"

"Quite a bit. I have kept him informed. He decided not to tell his closest friends about it. He is not sure who he trusts," Teagan said.

"How is Billy?" Jared asked. This meeting was the first time Jared had met Teagan.

Teagan studied Jared briefly, then said, "He's positive." Then Teagan smiled, "He wanted me to tell you not to feel bad about being unable to reach him when he fell from the bridge. He is worried that it has been eating at you. He wanted me to deliver that message."

Jared smiled and looked at Dorn and Raistlin, "Good old Billy Blaine."

Teagan had met Raistlin twice before that night and had kept in contact with Dorn since their first meeting. He genuinely respected all three men who shared the table with him and believed they trusted him. Raistlin had promised him land if he helped free the children. Teagan didn't care about the land. He wanted to be free of Lance and the town of Greystone. He wanted to defect. He would work in Raistlin and Dorn's lumber mill and live in the smallest shack in Ironwood to escape the evil he had seen. He felt like a genius; to accomplish this, he worked to get as close to Lance as possible. He was one of Lance's elites. It was the perfect espionage case, and he felt no guilt for doing it. If he could live on this side of the river and become friends with the great men who sat before him and start a family with Sky, he would do anything.

Chapter 56

One evening, while on the castle grounds, Teagan spotted a dog walking along the base of the castle ground curtain wall. It was odd because there were never dogs on the castle grounds; most were used for hunting and were kept in kennels at a private residence. Also, this one looked different from most of the hounds used in Greystone. He watched it for a few moments and spotted Billy sitting on a bench. Teagan walked to him and said, "Billy, have you seen that dog before?"

Billy looked up from a book he was reading, squinted to see better, and said, "It looks familiar, but I haven't seen it around here. I don't think I've seen a dog on the castle grounds before."

"Odd," Teagan said.

"Wait!" Billy said. "I think I know him." He set his book on the bench, stood up, and slowly approached the dog. "Atticus," he said as he got closer.

The dog turned, looked at him, and sniffed the air.

"Atticus, it's me, Billy."

Atticus wagged his tail and walked toward Billy. When he reached him, Billy began to pet him.

Billy looked at Teagan, "This is Atticus, Raistlin's dog that I told you about."

Teagan looked dumbfounded, "Didn't you say that was his dog when he lived in the other world?"

Billy nodded as he continued to pet the wire-haired Airedale.

"How is he here in Evergreen?" Teagan asked.

Billy looked at Teagan and said, "This must be his afterlife."

"Afterlife?"

Billy continued to look at Teagan, then said, "Probably a conversation for another time."

Teagan walked to the dog, patted it on the head, and looked at a tag hanging from its collar. The tag read "Atticus." "It is him, isn't it?" Teagan asked.

"It's him," Billy said as he patted Atticus on the head. "He's a bit younger than the last time I saw him, but it's him."

Teagan looked around for a moment, "I am going to see Dorn and Raistlin tomorrow evening. I should take him to Raistlin." He stooped down next to Billy and Atticus, "Billy, go to the kitchen and find some scraps, then take him and put him in an empty stable. I'll come and get him when I go to Ironwood."

Billy nodded and said, "Yes, sir."

#

Billy walked out of the castle with a wooden bowl in his hand; inside the bowl were a few pieces of roast, some carrots, and plenty of broth to wet the dog's whistle. He found Atticus in the same spot he had left him minutes before.

"C'mon, boy," Billy whispered. Atticus followed with his snout pointing toward the bowl in Billy's hand. Once they reached the stables, Billy found an empty stall and set the bowl on the dirt floor. Atticus began to eat the contents of the bowl. Billy walked out of the stall and closed the gate. He stood and watched the dog finish its meal.

"Hi, Billy."

Billy turned his head and saw Orla walking toward him. "Hi," he said.

She walked to him, looked in the stall, and asked, "Whose dog is that?"

"One of the guards wants me to keep an eye on him for a few days," Billy said. "Is it okay if I keep him here?"

"Sure," Orla said. "I'll make sure he has plenty of water."

They spoke for a few minutes, then Orla went on her way. Billy stayed for a bit and watched as Atticus went in circles. He found himself in a comfortable spot to lie in the straw bedding. Billy said goodnight to the dog and then walked toward the castle. The sun had already set, and the coolness of the night was in the air. He returned to the stall and unlatched the gate, leaving it open a few inches. Then he walked to the castle and his quarters.

Atticus napped for a bit in the stall, but once things got quiet and most of the sconces were extinguished, he nudged the gate open wider and walked out of his stall. He followed the wall on the outskirts of the castle yard until he reached the castle. He snooped around the castle until he found a door ajar. He put his snout through the opening, and the door opened wide enough for him to walk through. From here, he let his nose lead the way. The stone floor was cool on his feet, and the smell was musty when his nose was to the floor. When he raised his snout, he could smell lantern oil and a hint of smoke. He had a faint smell of the wolves with which he had fought. There were various scents in the air that he remembered from the fight: leather, pine, patchouli, and a touch of whiskey. The castle was quiet. Sconces on the walls were the only light. He kept his snout in the air and tried to follow the scents he remembered from the wolves.

Openings in the stone walls had stairways that led upward in a circle. When Atticus reached the third stairway, he began to walk up as quietly as possible.

There was a mix of dancing shadows from the low flame in the sconces as the stairs led up the circle. As he went around a few times, the smell of the wolves became stronger and stronger. He stopped when he saw someone standing at the top. Atticus was far enough down the stairs to remain in the shadows, so the guard didn't notice him. Atticus turned and walked back down.

He sat beside the bottom step for a spell. This was the stairway he needed. He wanted to go into the room at the top, but the guard was there, and Atticus was sure the guard would announce the dog's presence if seen. Atticus walked under the stairs and lay on the floor. He immediately noticed a hole in the wall. Several blocks were missing from the wall. The hole was barely enough for him to crawl through.

It was pitch black inside the hole, but dogs have excellent night vision. A second stairway led up the outside wall of the inner stairwell. It was a secret passage to the room above. A skinny person would have to walk up the stairs sideways to fit between the walls. Atticus walked up the stone stairs and went around twice as he ascended. Once he neared the top, he saw a glow. He slowly crept toward it. The light was coming through another hole in the wall, similar to the one at the bottom of the stairwell. Atticus crawled on his belly to see through the hole. The light came from a candelabra on a table in the middle of a large room.

The smell of the wolves he tangled with became stronger as he crawled through the hole. Once he was in the room, he lay still for a moment. The only sounds were the soft breeze that blew through a window and the gentle breathing of two people in bed. Atticus got to his feet and began to sniff around the room. The closer he got to the bed, the more the smell reminded him of the wolves he encountered at the Riverwalk. One arm was draped off the side of the bed; it belonged to the blond woman. He sniffed and walked around to the other side of the bed. The black haired man slept there. The smell of the wolves was profound. Atticus knew they were the people that had turned into wolves; he had watched it with his own eyes. They transformed as they fought with his master's friends in front of the arch at the Riverwalk. When he ran at them, they turned and tried to tear him apart, and they nearly did.

Even though he was a young and fit dog now that he was in Evergreen, he still knew he wouldn't have a chance against one wolf, let alone two. But a human? He could take a human. How he would have loved to jump on the bed and rip their throats out; he knew the consequences would far outweigh the joy of watching those two on the bed bleed to death. This was a new world to him; he wanted to discover it. He also had a feeling that his master was in this world, and he longed to find him. He put the urge to rest and sniffed around the room. A different scent reminded him of his old world; it only took a moment to find it. An arrow leaned against the bedpost. Its tip had flecks of gold that shined in the candlelight. He sniffed the arrow from its tip to its fletching. Many scents were associated with the arrow, but the strongest scent was his old world. The scents of the two people in the bed were strong on the arrow, but the smell of the old world was at its core.

Atticus lightly clamped his teeth around the shaft of the arrow. He had a relic from his old world; if he found his master, he would give it to him as a gift.

He padded back to the hole in the wall and crawled through. He went down the secret staircase and out of the castle without being seen.

#

Teagan walked up to the gate of Atticus's stall the next morning. The dog perked up its head from sleep when Teagan arrived. Next to the dog was an arrow. Teagan had heard about the legend of the arrow and what it looked like, and he knew what it was the moment he saw it. He opened the gate wider, walked into the stall, and bent down to pick up the arrow.

Atticus sat up and grabbed the arrow. As Teagan tried to get closer, Atticus began to growl at him.

"Okay, I see," Teagan said. "I think I know the person you want to give that to. I'll take you there later today."

# #

Atticus wouldn't let Teagan have the arrow, so as they walked through town, Atticus carried the arrow in his mouth. Most people didn't know the legend of the Crimson Arrow, and in the darkening of the evening, the arrow looked like any ordinary arrow to anyone who was paying attention. Teagan held his hat down low as he walked. Walking with the dog was an extra disguise for him; he never walked with a dog at his side before.

So, he strolled through Greystone unnoticed, walked across the bridge, made his way through Ironwood, and headed for the Barrow Homestead.

The lantern light made a rectangle on the grass outside the shed. The rectangle was bright, soft, and bright again from the flickering flame inside the glass.

He whistled softly so that the men in the shed would know he was approaching. He turned to Atticus and whispered, "Stay for a moment."

The dog sat on the ground, the arrow still in his mouth.

Teagan walked into the shed. Raistlin was packing tobacco into a pipe; an ale sat before him. Dorn sat across the wooden table from him. He was leaned back in his chair with a glass of whiskey in front of him. A bottle of whiskey and an empty glass also sat on the table, along with Raistlin's pouch of tobacco. Jared leaned against the wall.

Raistlin looked at Teagan from his seat and said, "Welcome back, my friend." The three of them had grown to like Teagan. They trusted him and had faith in him. If there were any doubt left, what was about to happen would make that disappear forever.

"Gentlemen," Teagan said and nodded. Dorn and Jared nodded back with friendly faces.

"Have a seat," Raistlin pointed to an empty chair. He pulled a match from his shirt pocket. "Ready for a drink?"

"In a moment," Teagan said. "I have something to show you."

Raistlin, Dorn, and Jared all looked at each other. "Okay," Raistlin said.

Teagan backed out of the doorway and looked to his right; he clicked his tongue twice and said, "C'mon boy."

Atticus walked into the dim light seeping out through the door. He walked through the doorway with the arrow in his mouth.

#

Atticus recognized the scents before he walked through the door. The three men in the shed were his friends, and one of them was his master. These people were friends with the boy who took him to the stable the evening before. It was all adding up, and if the man who had just walked him from the castle to here was friends with them, then they were a pack.

He looked at the three men as soon as he walked through the door. Two of them he recognized. The other was his owner; he recognized him by scent, but the man looked different. Atticus looked at his owner, wondering how he looked so different. Then his owner stood up and yelled, "Atticus!"

Atticus jumped onto the table, the arrow still in his mouth.

"Atticus!" Raistlin yelled again.

Atticus wagged his tail while he grunted, groaned, and snorted.

Raistlin held out his arms, and then Atticus dropped the arrow onto the table, wiggling with happiness; his tail went back and forth smoothly. He put his front paws on Raistlin's shoulders and began licking his face.

Raistlin hugged him and said, "Dreams do come true!"

The commotion knocked over Raistlin's mug of ale and pushed his tobacco pouch onto the floor.

Everyone smiled at the interaction, but one by one, they grew serious and looked at the arrow on the table.

Raistlin noticed the change in energy and said, "Hold on, buddy." He patted Atticus and gave the hand command for him to sit. Atticus immediately sat on the table. Raistlin looked at what everyone was gazing at. It was the Crimson Arrow. All of its legendary characteristics were there. The fletching was from a Great Horned Owl and was touched with oil. The shaft was made of Red Balau, and the arrowhead was made of quartz and zinc. On the tip of the arrowhead, specks of gold shimmered in the light from the lantern.

The room was silent; even Atticus stopped his panting and breathed normally.

"Teagan?" Raistlin asked. "How?"

Teagan shook his head, "I don't know," he said. "Atticus showed up last night. Billy figured out it was him, and we put him in a horse stall for the evening. When I checked on him this morning, he had the arrow with him and wouldn't let me touch it."

Raistlin picked up the arrow.

Atticus licked Raistlin on the cheek.

Raistlin looked at the others, "We need to make prototypes. We should start first thing in the morning. This arrow will only have one flight, and it has to be tried and true."

Chapter 57

The following morning, Raistlin, Dorn, and Jared began gathering things to make arrows identical in weight, balance, and sleekness to the Crimson Arrow. Since Red Balau was nearly impossible to find in Evergreen, Dorn went to the lumber mill and found a piece of Chengal that was comparable in weight. He ripped it down into many pieces, brought them back to the homestead, and began to shape them into shafts. Raistlin gathered every arrowhead he could find, and they separated only those that matched the size and weight closest to the one on the Golden Arrow. They trimmed the bird feathers to match the fletching as closely as possible. Dorn hafted the arrowheads to the shafts; by midday, they had six prototypes to practice with.

They walked down toward the barn with Atticus running ahead of them. Atticus had just met Lulu, Sally's dog, and was as excited as ever about his new life.

Hawley was in the clearing by the barn. Donte was behind him, pulling a wagon load of firewood. Atticus skidded to a stop on the dirt path when he saw the dragon. Dorn, Raistlin, and Jared stopped walking when the dog did. Atticus stood still except for slowly lowering his head. A growl came from him, and some of the hair on his back stood up.

Although still several dozen yards away, the dragon took notice. Donte stopped pulling the wagon and looked toward the dog. Hawley looked their way and smiled, unhooking the leather straps connected to the dragon.

"Easy, boy," Hawley said. "If that dog is friends with them, then he's friends with us, too."

Atticus took off toward the dragon in a full sprint. Raistlin laughed and said, "Better be careful, old buddy."

Donte dropped his head, and his eyes grew fierce. Atticus slid to another stop when he was just a toss of a stone's distance from him. They eyed each other up; the dragon was obviously much bigger than the dog. Atticus took a step forward, sniffing at Donte. Donte also took a step to help close the gap. Soon, they were nose to nose; the others watched with grins on their faces. When the dragon would move in the slightest motion, the dog would jerk but remain in place. Once Donte was satisfied with the meeting, he blew a burst of air out of his nose onto Atticus's face. The dog yelped and ran toward the three men with whom he had walked down the hill. Everyone laughed as Atticus took cover behind the men. Donte raised up and sat tall as if he was boasting.

They continued their walk to the barn. On the other side of the barn was an archery target. Dorn pointed the arrows in his hand toward the target, looked at Jared, and said, "You are the best shot here. Why don't we see how it goes."

Jared nodded and said, "I'll get my bow." He walked into the barn and grabbed his bow made of Yew, the same bow that Raistlin had given to him after he first arrived in Evergreen. How long ago that seemed to him; so many things had happened since that day.

While Jared began to launch arrows at the target, Atticus became more and more bold around the dragon. Soon, the dog was barking and chasing Donte's tail as the dragon playfully moved it back and forth.

Long before dinner, Jared had the arrows striking the target again and again. Every prototype flew the same, and no adjustments were needed from arrow to arrow. They hoped their calculations were accurate and the prototypes were identical to the Crimson Arrow. The Crimson Arrow could only be shot once, then it would disappear, regardless of whether it struck its intended target.

That evening, in the saloon, Dorn gave Jared his blessing over a whiskey. "I have longed to kill Lance Erikson," Dorn said. "But, if I don't have to deal with him in the remainder of the worlds I pass through, I don't care who kills him." Dorn held up his glass, "If you get a shot, take it. Banish him." Jared nodded, and they clicked their glasses together.

Chapter 58

Although Teagan was in Lance's fold, Boris consistently reported Teagan's doings back to Lance. Boris was Lance's true right hand; Teagan was in the fold because he wasn't trusted.

Boris watched from the upper branches of an oak tree as Teagan crossed the river into Ironwood. He usually went into the saloon, although he once took the road out of town that led to the Barrow Homestead. Boris coaxed one of the town's workers to help him spy. He was a builder in the town and a lonely young man. Boris often noticed that at the end of the day, the young man would walk home to a little hut on the north side of town and never go to the saloon in Greystone with the other workers.

"I am a swordsman from the castle," Boris said to the man one day as he approached him on his walk home from work.

The lad nodded, "I know. I've seen you around."

"Do you like your job?" Boris asked.

The lad shrugged his shoulders, "Sure."

"What do you like about it?"

"I like building things. Working with my hands."

"You know, Lance Erikson plans to add to his castle," Boris said.

"That so?"

Boris glanced in the direction of the castle. "It sure is." Then he looked back at the man. "Lance Erikson wants the best builders to build the addition. Two new towers connected by embattlements."

The man nodded.

"And he plans to pay well," Boris said. "He will even offer land to the master builders. I have watched you work. You could be a master builder on his castle."

The man's eyes lit up.

"I can make it happen, but I need a favor from you."

#

Two days later, Boris gave the young man instructions. "Walk across the bridge and into the saloon in Ironwood. Find a table near the man with the long hair and tattoos, whom I will have you follow. Try to hear everything said between him and whomever he speaks with."

"What if someone asks who I am?" The man's anxiety started to show.

Boris put a hand on his shoulder, "Tell them the truth. You are a builder from Greystone and wanted to get away from that town for a while. The worst they will do is kick you out and tell you to go back across the river. But they may also have some compassion. Ironwood is a peaceful town with nice people. But, wear your cap down like this," Boris pulled the man's cap down so it helped cover his face. "Teagan has likely seen you before. We don't want him to recognize you."

"What if he does?"

"You wanted to get out of town for a spell," Boris said. "Then I will need you to come back and tell me everything, and don't tell another soul."

The man nodded. Later that day, he headed across the bridge and became a spy.

Boris kept the man on a leash for several days in case he needed him again.

Even if there had been plans to add to the castle, it would never have come to fruition. Within weeks, Erickson's Castle would be destroyed.

#

Boris had a great vantage point from his tower window. With his spyglass, he could see things happen far away. Anyone he spied on had no idea they were being watched. On a few occasions, he was able to spy on Teagan and Sky. Jealousy always poked at him when he stumbled on their encounters, but it stabbed him in the heart when he watched them become more intimate.

Boris and Sky had been together only months earlier, but things didn't work out, and they called it quits. Boris had a hunch that Teagan and Sky were a couple, but they kept it a secret.

Boris had another spy, this one to whom he didn't have to make promises. It was gray with wings and the size of an oil lantern. He sent the bird down to a tree directly above the couple. The bird returned once Teagan and Sky gathered their things and went their separate ways.

It stood on the stone window sill and paced back and forth. "Shook! Shook!" were the sounds that came out. It was an imitation of Boris running a whetstone up and down his sword. The bird did it all the time. So much so that it nearly drove Boris up the wall.

"Enough shook, shook," Boris said. "What did you hear?"

"Meeting with townspeople," the bird said. Her phrases were short and straightforward, just like any other talking bird. "Free the children. Dorn and Raistlin."

"What else did you hear?" Boris asked.

"Billy Blaine."

"Billy Blaine?"

"Billy Blaine," it said again in its high-pitched voice.

Boris thought for a moment, then looked at the bird and asked, "Did you hear anything else?"

The bird began making kissing noises while continuing to pace back and forth on the sill.

Boris's face grew red, "Besides that!"

"Oh, Teagan!" the bird said. "Oh, Teagan!"

Boris roared in anger, grabbed the bird by the neck, and pulled it into the room. The bird squawked and squawked and flapped her wings. Feathers flew around the room. Instead of choking the bird to death, he threw it toward the other wall, knowing all well that the bird would take flight and avoid hitting the wall.

The bird did take flight and landed on a high bookshelf. She began pacing back and forth and said, "Oh, boy! Boris pissed!" Then she squawked. "Boris mad as a hatter! Boris madder than a rattlesnake!" She repeated the lines with squawks that exaggerated the expressions.

#

Like a good soldier, Boris reported all of his findings to Lance.

Lance leaned back in his padded chair and puffed his cigar. "I see."

"How is the project on the roof going?" Boris asked. "Will it be done if they attack soon?"

Lance blew his smoke toward the wooden rafters high above. "It is going beautifully. It will be done in no time."

Boris sipped his whiskey and set his cup on the wooden table between them. "Do you want me to kill Teagan?"

Lance looked at Boris, "Don't let your emotions get in the way."

"My emotions get riled up when I know someone is committing treason," Boris met Lance's eyes.

"You know what I mean."

"So?"

"Not yet," Lance flicked his ashes onto the stone floor. "We will find the perfect time."

Chapter 59

Billy's last glance at the outside world happened just a week after he had taken his previous curiosity tour of the castle and its towers. Once again, he traversed the stairs and looked out the window over the adjacent roof. Three catapults had been built. A heavy rope tied one back. The arm of the catapult bent back like the wood of a recurve bow.

Billy immediately knew he had to tell Teagan about this. They were preparing for battle. Lance somehow knew everything Teagan had been telling him. It was apparent that Lance was ready for a fight.

Billy ran down the stairs to find Lance standing at the bottom. Billy stopped on the third step. Lance stood with his arms crossed. Brenna and the blond swordfighter stood behind him.

"Billy, Billy, Billy," Lance said. "What shall we do with you?" Lance took two easy steps toward the stairs. "Have you ever heard the phrase, 'curiosity killed the cat'?"

Billy didn't respond; he only glared at Lance.

"Why do you snoop around my castle, Billy Blaine?" Lance leaned forward as he asked the question.

Again, Billy didn't respond.

"And the cat has your tongue," Lance said. "Guards! Take him down below! No outside privileges."

Chapter 60

Billy was given a new place to sleep, and his new dorm was in the castle's basement. He had hardly seen many of the kids that were in his quarters. The group he lived with before consisted of children who were responsible for everyday duties around the castle, such as cooking, cleaning, tending to the stables, and gardening. Now, the kids were either part of a hunting group or training to be swordsmen or archers. Many were doing all three. It was a focused group. They kept quiet and did precisely as they were told. Most of these children had been kidnapped from their homes in Greystone. On his first day in the basement, Billy tried to go outside when the last group was removed from their duties. One of the guards blocked the door and shook his head. Billy was returned to the kitchen, and a guard was always on watch.

On his second day, Teagan walked into the kitchen. It was just Billy and a guard. Billy was prepping vegetables; the guard was doing nothing. Teagan spoke with the guard briefly. The guard nodded and walked out the door.

Teagan approached Billy, "What the heck did you do?"

Billy shrugged.

"Don't just shrug at me," Teagan leaned closer to Billy. "Lance gave orders that you cannot leave the basement."

"I saw what they are building on the roof," Billy said.

Teagan gritted his teeth and looked at the ceiling for a moment.

"Did you know they were building catapults?" Billy asked.

"Yes, of course I did. I told you I always have the inside information."

"Why didn't you tell me?"

"Because it wouldn't do any good," Teagan said.

"Have you shared this with Dorn?"

"I have," Teagan nodded. "I told them to keep their eyes on the sky and stay under a copse of trees as they attack. It takes a long time to reload the catapults. They will almost be ineffective."

"Okay," Billy said and nodded. "Is there anything I should be doing?"

Teagan shook his head and said, "No, there is nothing you can do now. Things will be happening soon. When they do, I will unlock the door at the top of the steps on the other side of your quarters. When I do, I need you to run towards town. Greystone will be the safe haven. There are plenty of residents involved in this. Go there, and someone will keep you safe until we send you back to Ironwood."

Chapter 61

Dorn, Raistlin, Cambria, and Jared made final preparations. Raistlin would never have agreed to such a task a year prior, but today, with so many things having happened and things he had seen, he could no longer turn away from it.

A map of the castle and Greystone was rolled out before them. They had looked at the map in the past when they had to sneak past the castle to get Billy, Jared, and Josh back to their world. Only Billy and Josh made it back.

"We are going to attack them straight on," Raistlin said and pointed to the road that led to Greystone. "We will sneak across the river and quietly walk through town. The townspeople will follow us so they can receive their children." Raistlin placed both hands on the table and said, "I wouldn't get any of them involved in the fighting unless necessary. I don't want to be responsible for anyone's death." He pointed to the north side of the castle property, "We will have two dragons come in from this side. This is mostly just a scare tactic. We will come in from this side," he moved his finger to the east side of the property which was closest to Greystone. "We will have to keep cover under trees until we get past the castle walls. Once we are inside the battlements, the catapults won't get us; we will be too close. Teagan believes the catapults are to scare the townspeople. Lance thinks that they will all obey him again if he launches a rock into the town. Unless you launch a ball of fire, a catapult is useless anyway. It looks big and mighty, but it is nothing."

Raistlin leaned back and struck a match. He put the match to the bowl of his pipe and puffed several times until it lit. He blew cherry flavored smoke toward the ceiling. "Hunting parties will be out, so we will have less resistance," he said. "We will have to fight guards at the gates. Once we breach the battlements,

Teagan will unlock the door to the basement, and the children will be free. Our job is to protect them on their way out. I am sure there will be plenty of resistance."

"Brenna is mine," Cambria said. She leaned forward, grabbed Dorn's glass, and sipped his whiskey. "If we have to go toe to toe with Lance's cronies, I will take her."

"Lance is mine," Dorn downed the last whiskey in the glass. "I will finish this once and for all." He looked at Raistlin and said, "Raistlin, you have taught me in the past about how the people in Jared's world believe in Heaven and Hell." He slid his glass across the table and continued, "I hope Lance Erickson burns in Hell, and I hope his father is burning in Hell as we speak."

Silence engulfed the room until the sound of Raistlin pouring another glass for Dorn was heard. Even after the last drop was poured, the only sound was the spurts and sputters of the logs in the wood stove.

Chapter 62

As dusk approached, all of the things were put in place. Preston Thorton would watch the bridge from his usual fishing spot on his property on the river. Lanterns had been hung in the trees on each side of the river to possibly catch sight of someone who might try to swim across from the other side. Emily Thorton, Preston's wife and the sheriff of Ironwood, stayed in town with Sally. Raistlin, Dorn, Jared, Cambria, Theodore Johnson, and several people Theodore had recruited and trained with for several months walked across the bridge and took the road leading to Greystone. Raistlin and Dorn wore leather breeches and a leather vest over a long sleeved dark shirt. Jared wore the same but opted for a chain mail vest under the leather vest. It weighed him down a little but didn't hinder his movement. Since he had already been stabbed through the chest and barely survived, he had anxiety about going back into battle. The chain mail eased his fears a little. Cambria also wore leather pants and a long-sleeved leather top. Several throwing knives were packed in her vest, and a few small ones were tucked away in her boots. Her hair was pulled back into a French braid. She also wore chain mail under her top. Raistlin and Dorn opted to go without the chain mail. Jake had Donte and Zelda at the edge of the forest and would send them in as a scare tactic, nothing more. Once the main group reached town, some recruits would wait and gather the citizens. Torches would be lit, and they would parade to the castle walls to claim their children. Once Teagan saw the torches approaching, he would unlock the door to the stairs leading to the basement and lead the children out. Raistlin and company would have breached the gate and be inside the castle walls to fight resistance by this time.

Nobody from Greystone or Ironwood knew it, but the destruction of Erikson Castle was about to begin.

Chapter 63

Teagan and Sky stood in a copse of trees, looking at the castle. The sconces on the outer walls and the full moon made it easy to see everything.

"Once we see the torches coming from town, I will unlock the chain that locks the basement doors," Teagan said. He looked at Sky, "When I do, you head toward town. I will meet you. Billy will also meet us in town when he escapes the castle. We will grab our satchel and head toward Ironwood."

"That is it?" Sky asked.

Teagan nodded, "Yes, Dorn said I have done everything possible. We will be free. We can start our lives together without hiding anything."

She put her arm around his waist.

"Stay here," he whispered. "I am going to get closer to the gates." He walked several paces toward the gates and waited. The concrete walls were over a dozen feet tall, making it impossible to see the castle from his vantage point. The gates were wrought iron, only a few feet shorter than the concrete walls. The bars in the gate were spaced close enough together that an arm could barely pass through. The spaces in the gate allowed for a view inside the walls.

He heard some leaves rustle behind him and thought nothing of it, but when he heard a horse snort, he became curious.

Before he could turn around, Sky said, "Teagan!"

Teagan turned. A man stood behind Sky and held a knife to her throat. A horse stood next to them. Boris sat atop the horse with a bow across his lap; an arrow was nocked.

"You'll be in Greystone forever, Teagan," Boris said.

Before Teagan could do anything, the man jerked Sky's head back and ran the knife blade across her throat. Her attempt at a scream immediately turned into a gurgle, and blood splurted down the front of her tunic. The man pushed her down, and she fell face first to the ground. Boris raised the bow, pulled the string back, and released the arrow. The arrow shot into Teagan's chest and pierced his heart. He fell onto his back and didn't move. His dead eyes stared up at the star filled sky.

Chapter 64

Preston Thorton leaned against the tree while his horse was tied beside him. He rubbed the stump of a wrist that once had a hand attached to it many years ago. He heard a splash near the bridge. He looked in that direction and saw two horses with riders wading across the river to the Ironwood side. He hopped on his horse and trotted into town. He could barely see the riders going full sprint down the road that led to Barrow Homestead. He quickly rode to the sheriff's office and yelled for Sally. She and Emily Thorton came out.

"Two riders just crossed the river and are heading for the homestead," He said.

Sally nodded and looked at Emily, "Stay here." Then she untied her horse, climbed on, looked at Preston, and said, "Let's go."

#

A deer hide was draped and tied over the smokestack, blocking the smoke from the wood stove. The door and all three windows were nailed shut. Torches were lit and used to ignite the outside of the cabin. Then, the riders raced back down the road.

#

Tessa stopped Anastasia with her reading, "Shh." She thought she heard something on the roof. Then, there was banging on the windows and door. Smoke started to fill the cabin. Atticus began to bark.

"What is happening?" Nana had been knitting in the rocking chair but was now standing, her knitting project a heap on the floor.

Tessa grabbed the baby and put a cloth over his mouth. "Anastasia, here," and she gave Anastasia the other cloth. "Put it over your mouth."

She went to the door, but it wouldn't open. Nana checked the windows; they were also stuck shut. Nana broke the panes in one of the windows with the broom handle but was unable to break the mullions. None of them would be able to crawl through the window.

The smoke filled the cabin, enveloping them like a blanket.

"Get closer to the ground," Tessa told Anastasia. "We will have to crawl."

Flames began to lick up past the window sills. The logs crackled on the outside of the cabin. They crawled to the door, and Tessa sat up, tugging on the handle, but could not open it.

Moments later, they heard voices. It was Sally and someone else. Tessa couldn't place the male voice but had previously heard it. A loud thumping began on the other side of the door. Tessa backed away, and after the third thump, the door flew open. Preston Thorton came tumbling through. Smoke began to pour out the door, making it easier to breathe.

"Let's go," Preston said as he grabbed Anastasia and guided Nana out the door. Tessa ran after them with Sawyer in her arms; Atticus followed. They walked away from the cabin and watched it as it became completely engulfed in flames.

Chapter 65

Dorn, Raistlin, Jared, Cambria, Zed, Theodore, and a recruit who was handy with a sword approached the gate. A line of torches from the townspeople of Greystone weren't far behind them. Between the lantern light on the wall and the full moon, it wasn't hard to see two bodies on the ground several feet from the gate. Dorn pulled his sword as he approached, and the group followed behind him. Once he got closer to the bodies, he realized one of them was Teagan.

"Great Fathers," he whispered.

"Halt!" one of the guards yelled.

"Halt yourself," Raistlin said as he pulled his sword and approached the guards.

Both guards pulled their swords and faced off against Raistlin and Dorn. The guards had their backs to the gates. The steel started to clash, and their footwork was swift and precise. The others stood back, ready to fight. The quarters by the gate were too close for another to jump in and help; it would have made things worse. Both guards were quickly hurt and stripped of their swords. Jared quickly tied their hands together, and the guards sat back to back, unable to do anything except yell for help.

People within the walls scurried around at the commotion.

The gate was quickly opened, and they all entered, leaving the guards sitting outside the walls. Cambria caught a motion from above. A guard was atop the rampart; he nocked an arrow and pulled the string back. He aimed down at the men leading the group.

"Halt!" He yelled.

Cambria pulled a knife and launched it end over end. Before it struck the man in the shoulder, it sliced through the bowstring, causing the bow to break with a loud crack. The man let out a yell and stumbled, the blade still sticking out of his shoulder.

Jared quickly climbed the ladder up the rampart; his bow was in his hand, and a quiver of arrows slung over his shoulder. When he reached the top, he pushed the wounded man over the wall into the bushes below. Then he faced the courtyard and knocked an arrow.

Some people were running toward the castle for shelter, while others were coming out to see what the commotion was about. Boris and three other swordsmen walked from the corner of one of the outer walls. They met the group head-on with their swords drawn.

"Where is Lance?" Raistlin asked.

"What business do you have here?" Boris countered.

"Why is that man dead just outside the gate?" Raistlin asked.

"We executed him for treason," Boris said.

"I order you to release the children that Lance has kidnapped over the last few years," Raistlin said.

Boris laughed, "Not a chance. Not to mention, I don't take orders from you."

"Then this is how it will be," Raistlin said, pulling his sword. The rest of the group drew their swords. The two groups seemed to spread out and match up. Not having a sword, Cambria backed away and scanned the castle grounds. Raistlin faced off against Boris. One of the men with Boris stepped before Dorn and took a defensive stance. The matchup was five to four in favor of Raistlin's group. The men defending Erikson's castle were excellent sword fighters. They were so good that the one who had to take on two because of the imbalance held his own for several minutes.

Boris was a great fighter. Even young Raistlin had his hands full. Swords clashed and flashed in the torchlight.

Cambria went to the double door that angled against the ground; a stairway would be on the other side when they opened it. A chain looped through the handles was connected by a large lock. Cambria pulled a knife and tried to pick the lock. She continually glanced around as she fiddled with the mechanism.

Dorn struck his opponent and wounded him enough that the young man staggered backward, dropped his sword, and held his hand out in surrender. Dorn grabbed the man's sword and backed away from the fighting. He tossed the sword aside and went to Cambria.

"I can't unlock it," she said.

"Stand back," Dorn said. He positioned himself over the doors. He raised his sword high above his head and struck the lock. The chain jumped from the strike. He struck again and again. He heard a familiar voice yelling from above.

Both Dorn and Cambria looked up. Billy Blaine stood on the top of the wall that extended up nearly forty feet. He was looking back toward the roof and pointing as he yelled. Then he turned and jumped off the wall, hurtling toward the ground faster and faster.

Chapter 66

Just as Billy was ready to settle into bed, the doors to the quarters crashed open. Two guards walked into the room. One of them bellowed, "Billy Blaine!"

Billy stayed silent as he sat on his bed. All of the guards knew who Billy Blaine was. They walked to the end of his bed.

"Come with us," one of them said.

After Billy refused to move, one of the guards grabbed him and pulled him off his bed. The other guard grabbed his free arm, and they led him to the door.

The guards stayed silent as Billy bickered away about the situation. They walked him to a stairway that he had never seen on his previous excursions of the castle and dragged him up the stairs. Once they were at the top, they opened a door and pulled him through.

Billy stood before the project that he had seen through a window in another stairwell just days earlier. Now, it all made sense. Looking at the completed contraptions allowed him to put the puzzle together. Three skinny trees had been transformed into individual launching devices. The tree trunk was bolted to a turret on the flat roof. Metal bars were wrapped around the trunks and extended to the turret, allowing the tree to stand vertically. A wooden basket was attached to the top of each tree. Ropes were attached just below the baskets. The catapult in the middle was facing the mountains north of the castle. Two men pulled on the rope and pulled the tree back far enough that it touched the roof of the castle that they stood upon. They wrapped the rope around one of the anchor points scattered across the roof to hold the catapult in place. They struggled to roll a large boulder into the basket. Once the boulder was in the basket, they waited. The sounds of swords clashing could be heard from below.

"Release!" One of them yelled.

The base of the anchor was struck with a large hammer. This caused the rope to slip off the top of the anchor, and the catapult was released. The tree trunk snapped forward, launching the large boulder into the air. The boulder sailed into the hills on the north side of the castle. The men immediately began to pull the catapult back, and another boulder was rolled to them.

Billy saw movement in his peripheral vision. He looked to his left, and there stood Lance. Billy rolled his eyes.

"Billy Blaine," Lance said, "Fancy meeting you here. Did you come up for the view?"

"Not by choice," Billy said.

"Well," Lance looked at him. "Hold on now. I ordered my guards to bring you up here. It was my choice to do that. So, by rights, you did come here by choice. My choice," he laughed.

"That's very philosophical," Billy snarked.

"Billy, you are mine forever. We should consider ourselves brothers," Lance smiled.

Billy rolled his eyes again.

"Can you hear the swords, Billy?" Lance asked. "Those are your friends. They are fighting for you."

"You will never beat them."

"Oh, Billy. Don't be so negative," Lance said.

"Dragons!" One of the guards yelled before Lance could continue.

In the distance, the silhouettes of two dragons were seen coming from the edge of the mountains.

"Load the next catapult," another of them yelled.

Two began pulling back another catapult arm while the others focused on the approaching dragons.

The person who seemed to be in charge stood directly in front of the turret and lined himself up with the dragons in the distance. "Adjust as needed."

Two of them adjusted the turret so the arm of the catapult aligned with the man in charge and the dragons.

The man moved to the side and said, "Wait!"

They waited for several seconds, then he said, "Release!"

The boulder launched out of the basket and disappeared from the glow of the sconce lights on the castle walls. The silhouettes of the two dragons were visible, and after a few moments, the outline of the boulder became visible above the horizon of the mountains. The two dragons and the boulder grew closer and closer together. The smaller dragon suddenly moved, but the bigger dragon wasn't quick enough. The boulder struck the bigger dragon, and the beast swirled to the ground.

"No!" Billy screamed. He looked up at Lance and yelled at him, "Why are you so evil? What is the matter with you?" He pointed toward the edge of the roof and said, "I hope they kill you when you go down there to fight! I hope they put your head on a post!"

Then Billy started to push Lance. He pushed him again and again, but Lance just stepped back for a moment and laughed. Billy began to punch him in the stomach. One of the guards tried to grab him, but Billy squirmed out of his grip and ran across the flat roof. He jumped onto the parapet and spun around on agile feet. Another boulder was launched.

"You will never win, Lance! I hope you never get anything you want. I know one thing: I will never exist in this world with you. Goodbye!"

Then Billy spun back around and jumped off the roof. He spread his arms out and closed his eyes. He wondered what hitting the ground would bring him this time. The first time he fell was in the In Between; he remembered struggling to escape Lance's grasp. Dorn came to the rescue that time. The second time he fell was from the bridge, also from the In Between. That time, he figured he would get smashed onto the rocks. It was a disappointing thought because they had rescued Raistlin and were going back to Evergreen. He had always worried about their heartbreak until he found out that Teagan had told them he was still alive. Now, he wondered what was on the other side of this fall. The thoughts that can go through one's head quickly: Would he wind up back in his world? Would he be with his daughter again? Would he be with Anna? He welcomed the thoughts.

Part VI: Endings

Chapter 67

Zelda and Donte were commanded by Jake to fly to the castle. They left from the edge of the forest. They flew through the air towards the glow of lights from the castle grounds. Zelda flew back and forth, scouting the area. She had excellent night vision and scanned the ground for any trouble. A movement from the castle distracted her from looking at the ground. Something significant had moved quickly. Suddenly, a large boulder was hurtling toward them. She dove out of the way, but Donte wasn't quick enough. The boulder struck him in the side. The sound of breaking bones could be heard as his wing was crushed. The impact sent him spiraling to the ground. He landed on the rocky terrain with a thump and remained motionless.

Zelda dove down and circled over Donte; he lay on the rocks in a heap. In anger, Zelda darted up and flew toward the castle. She could hear someone yelling, a familiar voice she hadn't heard in months. She also heard the clash of metal. Torches lined the trees outside of the castle walls. As she flew closer, she saw the commotion on one of the lower flat roofs. A young boy ran across the roof. She immediately recognized him as Billy Blaine. It looked like he was racing to the roof's edge to jump off. She flew as fast as she could but knew there was no way she would make it if he jumped. Billy stopped at the roof's edge, turned, and yelled something back at the others. Another boulder was launched, and Zelda barely dove out of the way to avoid it. The speed of it flying by her put her in a whirlwind for a moment, but she quickly recovered. She continued toward the castle. Metal flashed in the torch lights as a group fought with their swords. Dorn was at the door, smacking it with his sword; Cambria was beside Dorn, scanning the area.

Then Billy jumped off the roof.

Zelda swooped down and tried to get Billy before he hit the ground, and miraculously, she succeeded. She nabbed him with her mouth. She held him by the shoulder. Billy yelled at first, then had excited exclamations when he realized it was Zelda. She lowered him to the ground and released Billy onto the grass in the courtyard.

He looked around for a moment, then Dorn yelled to Billy and pointed toward the open gate, "Go, Billy! Go to town! You'll be safe!"

Billy turned and ran towards the gate.

Dorn began to beat on the chain again. Zelda watched him hit it a few times, then nudged him out of the way. Dorn stood to the side as Zelda took the chain in her mouth and yanked. It only tugged on the doors. She pulled again, with the same result, except this time there was a slight give, as if things had stretched out. On the third yank, the chain broke into pieces, sending shards of metal flying. She grabbed one of the door latches in her mouth and ripped the door off the hinges; she did the same with the other.

When the stairway was exposed, teenage children were at the bottom of the stairs, screaming.

Zelda looked to the roof and took flight.

Chapter 68

Once Zelda took flight, Dorn raced to the sword fight, and Cambria descended the first two steps to the basement and soothed the teens.

"It's okay, it's okay," she said. "Don't be afraid of the dragon. You all can go home now." She walked back to the top of the stairs, but the children stayed below. "Come up, please. You can trust me." She pointed to the torches outside the castle walls and said, "Your family is out there right now. We've worked out a plan to set you all free. Now is your chance."

A few of the children whispered to each other. Cambria made another plea, and a few hesitantly walked up the stairs and looked around. Once the others saw them speed off, they ascended the stairs, two or three at a time. Soon, children ran to the gate; most of them emerged from the basement, while others came out through the castle's other doors. The children that had been kidnapped from Greystone raced to the gate, excited to be reunited with their families. The others that Lance captured from the In Between walked toward the gate, unsure what to do. They looked lost. A few of them looked back at the castle, wondering if they should return.

Some families outside the gate witnessed what was happening and yelled to the confused children. Eventually, all the children, including those from Greystone and beyond, were taken off the castle grounds and to safety.

Chapter 69

Zelda took flight and flew straight up to the parapet. She realized the boulder that had sent Donte to the ground came from the wooden contraptions before her. Everyone on the roof scrambled for the door to the stairwell the moment they saw Zelda land on the parapet. Lance was the first to disappear. Unfortunately, some didn't make it off the roof before Zelda scorched it. She heaved a stream of fire, and all three catapults and two of Lance's men were instantly engulfed in flames. They scrambled and waved their arms around, which allowed the fire to grow. The catapults and the wooden surface of the roof were an inferno. One of the men staggered to the roof's edge and fell off in a ball of fire.

Zelda turned around on the parapet and looked at the grounds before her. She extended her neck and let out a roar. Her claws gripped the top of the wall; the stone beneath them started to crumble and fall to the ground. She shot a line of flames and scorched the treetops outside the castle walls.

Zelda was out of sorts. She was always the peacekeeper amongst the dragons, a mama of sorts. When she saw Donte fall, things changed; something snapped. She roared again; this time, it was louder than ever. The children, along with many of the adults, put their hands to their ears. Her eyes were fierce as she leaned forward on the parapet and looked at the commotion below.

Chapter 70

Once Zelda ripped open the doors to the basement and Cambria got the children out, Dorn ran to the fight. Their recruit was crawling away from the conflict with a wound to his side; blood stained the ground as he dragged himself away. Raistlin was still fighting with Boris. Two of Lance's fighters ran back into the castle; they feared the dragon's roars and fire.

Dorn looked up at the castle and yelled, "Lance Erikson! Come out here, you coward. Come out here and face your death." Dorn walked in a circle, scanning his surroundings. He looked up and down, and once he made a full circle, he saw movement from the far corner of the castle.

Lance walked out of the castle with his sword in hand. Dorn waited for him to approach, and then they faced off. Their swords clashed. The battle had begun.

All the other fighters except Raistlin and Boris stopped fighting to watch the rematch between the foes from opposite sides of the river. Townspeople at the edges of the castle grounds with their long-lost children inched closer to watch the fight.

Four of the best sworders in Evergreen fought in pairs at the base of Erikson's Castle. Although it would end quickly, it was an event that would become folklore for decades to come.

Dorn and Lance fought with fervor. Their swords flashed in the light of the sconces, and their feet moved with ease and grace. Over and over, a sword attack from one or the other was blocked with a clash of metal. Only a few strikes slipped by. Lance caught Dorn in the side; the move sliced through Dorn's leather vest and cut him to the ribs. Dorn hardly grimaced as blood began to seep through the cut in his vest. Dorn jabbed his weapon forward to return the favor, and had Lance not turned his upper body to avoid the attack; it may have killed him. Instead, he spun completely around, and their swords clashed again. Both men began to sweat, and neither knew they were about to reach their fate.

In the last moments of Dorn's life, he fought like a master swordsman. Blood continued to seep out of his side, but the wound failed to dull his movements. His hands were fast, and his feet moved as if he were dancing on air. It was gallantry in the truest sense.

#

Jared had an arrow knocked the entire time the commotion was happening. He saw Billy jump off the wall and get caught in midair by Zelda. He saw the kids run up the stairs and out of the castle after Cambria pleaded with them to do so. There were no shots to take with his bow. Except for their one recruit being injured, the fighting was either even or in their favor. On two occasions, he had Boris in sight, but Raistlin was moving quickly, and Jared could not get a clean shot. Once Lance walked out of the castle, Jared took the arrow and put it back in the quiver, and he pulled out the Crimson Arrow and knocked it. Once again, he could not get a shot since Lance and Dorn immediately started fighting.

Jared longed to be down on the ground fighting. Seeing the castle grounds and Lance again made him burn with rage. Lance had nearly killed him when they cut through the castle grounds in the past to try to find passage to the other world. Maybe it was foolish for Jared to be fighting such a seasoned swordsman at the time.

#

While Dorn fought, he saw a movement on the side of the castle. Tucked away on the side of the closest tower was a small balcony. The motion he detected was Brenna walking through a door and onto the balcony. She had her long bow with her; she knocked an arrow. Brenna pulled the string back, bending the wooden bow. Dorn looked in the direction she was aiming. Cambria had just come up the stairway from the basement and was scanning the courtyard to ensure no more children were around. Cambria was the target.

Dorn backed away from Lance and began to run, shifting his vision from Cambria to Brenna. He yelled Cambria's name. He dropped his sword. Cambria turned her head toward Dorn. Dorn glanced back up at Brenna while he ran. Brenna released the arrow. Cambria looked, wondering why Dorn was racing toward her. Dorn dove with his hands outstretched. He took the pose of a goalie trying to block a penalty kick in a soccer match in the other world. He was facing the balcony while he was in the air. He could see the arrow flying. The arrow penetrated his chest and shot through his heart. He died instantly.

Cambria looked up at the balcony and saw Brenna knocking another arrow. In quick succession, Cambria threw two knives. Both knives stuck in Brenna's chest. She dropped her bow, which snapped in two when it hit the stone walk below the balcony. She fell forward, and her body folded over the side of the balcony. Her arms and hair dangled.

Cambria turned to Dorn and screamed. She kneeled next to him and administered any first aid she could.

#

Jared was confused when Dorn ran from the fight, but in a matter of seconds, Dorn was dead. Jared turned back to where Dorn had just been fighting, and he saw Lance standing with his sword in his hand and a smile on his face.

Jared pulled the bow back; the flecks of gold in the arrow's tip sparkled in the light from the sconces. He released the string, and his shot was as good as any shot he had ever taken. The arrow pierced Lance's chest. Lance immediately fell backward, arched his back, and held his hands to the arrow in his chest. After a few seconds, he stopped moving. The Crimson Arrow faded to nothing. Lance Erikson lay dead on the ground with a small hole in his chest. The legend of the arrow was true; it could only be shot once, and then it would disappear for decades, maybe even centuries.

Raistlin and Boris stopped fighting, then Boris turned and ran back into the castle.

Chapter 71

Once Zelda saw Dorn go down, she dropped from the roof to the ground. She looked at the spot from which the arrow came. She shot flames toward the balcony, but Brenna was already dead. Flames covered the wooden door, and Brenna's hair caught fire a moment before the rest of her body. Smoke from the burning door met smoke from the burning roof. It created a dark cloud that hung over the castle, blocking the view of the night sky.

Zelda roared again and walked toward where the group had been swordfighting moments before. Boris had already left, and the rest of his group immediately ran into the castle. Zelda went to a set of double wooden doors at ground level and banged her head on them. She banged again. The door splintered. She kept hitting it until it was open enough for her mouth to fit. She yanked on one of the doors and ripped it off its hinges. She did the same with the other door. She was just small enough to squeeze through the arched opening.

Once she was inside the castle, she raised her head and roared. Any adults left in the castle scrambled for cover. A few of them took to the circular staircases that led up the towers. Zelda shot a stream of fire into the base of the stairwell. The flames chased up the tower steps. Screams could be heard from the unfortunate ones who chose to take those stairs. She breathed fire through the great hall of the castle. Every table, shelf, and cupboard was engulfed in flames. She shot more fire toward the rafters above and into more stairwells. Smoke gathered under the rafters, and the fire spread under the roof. She poked her head into rooms and shot flames. In between the flame shots, she roared.

A dragon would do anything for its master. It was too much once Zelda saw Dorn get killed after seeing Donte get knocked out of the sky. She knew what she had to do. Even if it was a suicide mission, she knew this was the only way to destroy the castle and everything Lance Erikson had ever loved. She would stay in the castle until it was achieved.

Zelda was quite possibly the most loyal and beautiful being in Evergreen. Her eyes made her look like a dream. It was a brilliance that all others wanted to be around, but now those eyes had darkened and filled with overwhelming sadness and fury.

The rafters began to creak and buckle as the fire weakened the roof's strength. The burning rafters and roof planks crashed onto the poor dragon.

Chapter 72

When the dragon breached the castle, Boris was at a loss. The highest ranks were gone. He had killed Teagan, and now Lance and Brenna were gone. He had nowhere to go, no one to turn to. He was done. He slipped into one of the bedrooms when Zelda reached the main hall. He would burn with the castle; it was the only way.

The heat in the room rose rapidly as the dragon sprayed fire throughout the main hall. Boris sat in a nearby chair and closed his eyes, debating whether to stay in the room or run into the main hall to end it sooner.

"Hey," someone near him whispered. The whisper was between dragon roars; otherwise, Boris would never have heard it. "Hey!" it said again, louder this time.

Boris opened his eyes. A short man in a robe stood before him. Boris stood and jumped back.

"Don't be afraid," the man said as he stepped forward. "I won't hurt you." He held out his hand to Boris.

"Who are you?" Boris asked in a shaky voice.

The dragon roars were getting more frequent, so the man had to yell. "My name is Asmund Edmund. I can help you."

"How?" Boris asked.

"Come with me," he said. "I know a way out." Asmund grabbed his hand and led Boris into the great hall. The dragon's back was to them as it sprayed flames to the rafters. They snuck into the next stairwell before the dragon had a chance to notice them. Asmund raced up the spiral stairs, and Boris followed. They ran through the room at the top of the stairs. The fire had spread to the roof above the room they were in. They hurried out of the room onto a balcony. The balcony was a few feet from the sheer stone wall that went two hundred feet over their heads.

"There is nowhere to go from here," Boris yelled.

Asmund held up his hand for a moment. A walkway appeared before them. It was connected to the balcony, and the other was attached to the stone wall. Slowly, an arch appeared at the end of the walkway.

Asmund jumped over the short balcony wall and onto the walkway, "Let's go," he said.

"Where?" Boris yelled.

"To other worlds," Asmund said. "Come with me." Then he ran across the walkway and into the arch. His sandals were visible as he ran.

Boris looked up at the burning roof of the castle, then he leaped over the wall and followed the traitor, Asmund Edmund, into the arch.

The arch faded and disappeared, and then it was just the stone wall again as if the arch had never been there. They were never seen in Evergreen again.

Chapter 73

They could hear screams within the castle and Zelda's roars while Cambria worked on Dorn. She tried several things to revive him, but it was no use. Dorn was dead. Cambria looked up at her father and shook her head, then broke down crying and put her head on Dorn's chest.

Raistlin, Jared, Zed, and Theodore looked around in disbelief. The courtyard was empty except for a few townspeople coming through the gate to see what had happened. Smoke was coming out of all of the castle windows. Moments later, the main roof was burning. The screams in the castle grew quiet, but Zelda's roars could still be heard. Once the castle roof caved in, the dragon's roars stopped.

#

One of the townspeople pulled his horse and buggy into the courtyard. They loaded Dorn onto the back of the wagon. The castle was obliterated to just stone walls. Embers glowed from inside, the last remnants of a fire that changed the future of so many lives.

By the time they left the castle grounds, daylight was showing itself in the eastern skies. The wounded recruit rode on the seat next to Raistlin. The rest of them, along with Billy Blaine, followed behind the wagon on foot. On the road through Greystone, the residents and their children lined the sides of the streets and stood in silence as they passed.

Some townspeople gasped and pointed; a glow from the castle lighted their faces. They all turned around, and triumph filled their hearts for a moment. Zelda was streaking straight up into the sky. Embers fell from her body, creating a spectacle of bright, glowing colors behind her. She let out a roar as she flew. Parts of her body glowed like hot coals glow in a dying fire. Then she flew into the black cloud that hovered over the castle. Now and then, they could get a glimpse of her glowing spots. She was flying toward the mountains.

Chapter 74

Tessa, Nana, Sally, Anastasia, Atticus, and Lulu waited near Sally and Dorn's porch. Raistlin and Tessa's cabin was a pile of ashes except for the stone chimney that still stood in the morning mist. The chimney towered like a ghost; the mist distorted its mortar lines. Once the sun broke over the horizon, the mortar lines could be seen again. The morning shined its beauty over a land that, in one night, had been changed forever.

They heard the clop of hooves and looked toward the road from town. Two horses pulled a wagon. They didn't recognize the horses, but they knew the people. They looked closely to find all of their loved ones. Their observations suggested that something was wrong, but no one mentioned it.

Raistlin stopped the wagon. Those who had been walking behind the wagon stopped without a word. Raistlin stepped down from the wagon. He looked at Tessa and then lowered his head.

Sally approached the wagon slowly. The look on everyone's face answered the question she dreaded to ask. Once she could see over the sides of the wagon, she let out a scream that sent chills down the spines of everyone there. She climbed onto the back of the wagon, screaming "No" over and over again. She wailed as she hugged her dead husband. All of them looked away. Cambria began to sob. Tessa buried her face in Raistlin's chest. Anastasia wept. Billy Blaine's eyes were swollen and red from crying through the night.

Later that morning, Raistlin began to make a casket for his friend.

Chapter 75

Evergreen folklore says that dragons are resilient and very tough to kill. Typically, dragons die of old age. The murder of Celeste was an exception to the rule. The slumber sand put her and Donte in a vulnerable situation in the barn. An entire roof, even a flaming roof, falling onto the back of a dragon doesn't automatically mean death. Dragons are nearly fireproof.

The roof fell onto Zelda, but it didn't crush her. The flames were all around her; a burning rafter was lying on her back. She squirmed and fought to get out from underneath the glowing rubble. She climbed atop the pyre once she could push the burning wood aside. She flew up through the castle's great hall and ascended out where the roof once was. A plume of dark smoke surrounded her as it took the same path to the sky as she did. She flew straight up until she was above the smoke of the burning castle, and then she flew toward the mountains.

She found Donte, flew down to the ground, and lay beside him. She was burnt and exhausted.

She woke with the sun shining. She got to her feet. The scorched parts of her body were tight and stiff. She nudged Donte. He stirred for a moment and went still. She nudged him again. He woke, raised his head, and looked around. He tried to get to his feet but collapsed. After a few more attempts, he could stand but couldn't lift one of his wings. They slowly made their way toward home.

Two days later, they reached the group of people that lined the road, Zelda realized what was happening. Donte would figure it out when they reached Rickenback Mountain, and he would also have a broken heart to mend.

Chapter 76

Two days after the battle, they lined the road that led to the mountain. Raistlin led the procession on foot with Atticus by his side. Tessa directed the horses that pulled the first wagon. Sally was by her side, and Dorn's casket was in the back. Lulu lay stretched out next to the casket. Jake walked behind Dorn and Lulu. All the remaining dragons, in single file, followed Jake. Jared and Cambria were in the next wagon, with Billy and Anastasia in the back. Hawley, Zed, and Theodore followed with their wagons, and many others from town followed on foot.

As the procession started moving, Billy jumped to his feet and yelled, "Look! Dragons!"

Anastasia stood next to him and then stretched onto her tippy toes to try to see. Everyone turned. Two dragons were slowly making their way up the hill. It was Donte and Zelda. Zelda's beautiful face was scarred and burnt. Many areas on her body were black and scorched. She moved slowly next to Donte. Donte could barely walk, and one of his wings was lame and broken, dragging on the ground alongside him. They made their way to the back of the procession.

Raistlin watched the dragons approach, and when they stopped at the back of the procession, both dragons looked his way. Raistlin nodded, turned back around, and began walking up the road.

The procession followed as they made their way to Rickenback Mountain to bury their friend. At the back of the procession, a line was left in the dirt road from Donte's wing dragging beside him.

#

Raistlin, Hawley, Zed, and Jared carried the casket to the grave. The wooden cover hadn't been put on yet. Dorn was dressed in leather breeches and a matching vest. Under the vest, he wore a long-sleeved, white cotton shirt. His hands rested on his torso, fingers laced together. It looked as if he was taking an afternoon nap. There were no miracles when Dorn was mortally wounded. Nothing Cambria had ever learned as a medicine woman would have cured him. In this world, he would rest at the base of Rickenback Mountain. In the next world, he would embark on a new adventure.

Raistlin walked to the wagon and pulled something wrapped in leather. He held it in his arms as he walked back to the casket. He stood and looked down at his friend. Everyone grew still. Both dogs lay behind Raistlin as he began to speak.

"When you are best friends with someone, one of you will have the sorrow of burying the other," he spoke loudly so everyone could hear. "Dorn was tough, stoic, and gallant. He defended anyone he called a friend and never gave up." Many in the crowd began to cry. Sally fell to her knees and sobbed. Raisltin kept speaking; his voice never wavered. "When I was trapped in another world for thirty years, I never gave up hope. I knew, one day, I would come back to Evergreen. I knew Dorn would come and find me."

Raistlin pulled the leather from the object in his hands. It was Dorn's sword. It had been polished to a sparkle since the battle. Raistlin stepped forward and placed it across Dorn's chest. He moved Dorn's hands so they held the sword close.

"Dorn Hale, you were like a brother to me. I will never meet a stronger or more loyal person." Raistlin's eyes started to well with tears. "Here in Evergreen, I have spent nearly every day of my life with you, and I would do it all again, my friend." He reached down and put his hands on Dorn's, "Take this sword with you to the next world. Use it to protect yourself and those you love. I will see you when I get there." Raistlin took a step away from the casket.

Sally stood and brushed the dust off her knees. She leaned down and put her head on his chest. She sobbed a few more times, then regained her composure. She kissed him on the lips, then stood and took a step back. She looked at Zed and Hawley and nodded.

Zed and Hawley placed the lid on the casket and began to hammer nails into it. The dragons turned away from the grave and faced the countryside. Brutus was the first to let out a roar; then, it was Alonzo and Dorian. The three dragons roared in unison. Although it took the last two dragons everything they had to roar in their injured states, Zelda and Donte contributed. The roars let the next world know that Dorn Hale was coming.

The beasts bellowed their sorrow into the sky for nearly a minute. Tears flowed from everyone. Billy Blaine covered his face with his hands and bawled uncontrollably.

All the dragons stopped roaring simultaneously, and their echoes slowly rolled across the land and disappeared.

Anastasia whispered in Billy's ear, "I love you, Billy Blaine."

Epilogue

Hickory, Ohio

Spring 2032

Samira entered Josh's office, and her baby bump showed through her summer dress. Willy followed her. He leaned against Samira's leg while he sucked his thumb. Willy was three, and he was their first child. Now, the second one was on the way. Their Airdale Terrier sat next to them. Their first Airedale, Atticus, was a rescue from an old man in Detroit. They loved the breed so much that when Atticus passed, they went out and found an Airedale puppy. They named her Scout.

Their dreams had come to fruition. After Josh's accident and recovery, he continued working toward his degree in Veterinary Medicine. She changed her major from Dentistry to Business Administration and graduated before he did. They moved to Hickory after finishing school. They started their own veterinary business. Initially, it was limited to house calls for larger animals, such as horses and goats. They built their own house on Josh's family's farm. Then, they built a clinic in town and operated it.

"My Mom and Dad are taking Willy for the night. I'm going to run him up there and have dinner with them, then I'll be back home," Samira said. "You want to come with us?"

"Ah," Josh said. "I've got some stuff to go through. I'll make myself a sandwich. Maybe we can watch a movie when you get back."

She sat on his lap and said, "Maybe so." She kissed him on the forehead, "Maybe no." She winked at him and stood. She looked at Willy and said, "Give Daddy a hug; we have to go."

As Willy ran to him and hugged him, Josh said, "Do you think we will always call him Willy, or maybe Will at some point?"

"When he becomes a veterinarian, lawyer, or an oil tycoon, William Jared Collins will be what they call him," she said.

"That does have a nice ring to it, doesn't it," Josh said as he kissed his son on the forehead, "Be good, Willy. I'll see you tomorrow."

"Bye, Daddy."

"I love you," Josh said.

He watched them go out the door. He lifted his pant leg as high as possible and removed his prosthetic. It was from an injury he had ten years before. A crazy driver drove onto the sidewalk and hit him. The driver was never found. He set the prosthetic next to his desk and rubbed his stump. He reached onto a shelf behind him and pulled down a glass and a bottle. He poured himself a bourbon and set the glass next to the keyboard of his computer. Scout plopped down in the dog bed next to Josh's desk.

Josh clicked through a few screens and then opened a blank document. He looked at the empty page and sipped on his bourbon. He leaned back in his office chair and thought to himself. He looked at a picture of his brother that hung on his wall.

The cursor blinked on the page.

Next to the keyboard was a small purple book with black trim. Although it resembled a journal, it was called the Book of Secrets. It was a book he begged his mother to buy him when he was twelve. A few days after he acquired it, he learned it had magic. It helped Josh and Jared navigate their way to Evergreen. After that first visit to Evergreen, Josh lost the book. A decade later, Samira had given it to him when he came home from the hospital. The book quickly found its way into a box in a closet. During a move from one apartment to another, Josh saw the book. He put it on the nightstand at the new place. The first few evenings, there were blank pages when he opened the book. As he considered packing it away again, words appeared on the page when he opened it on the fourth night. He sat up a little from his lying position on the bed. His mouth dropped open as he read. He turned the book toward Samira so she could see. The words instantly disappeared. It was weeks before they returned to the page, so the book was meant only for Josh.

What he read were things that were happening in Evergreen. There were stories of Dorn and Raistlin as children and teens. Stories of him and Jared arriving in Evergreen. A tale of Billy Blaine falling from a bridge to meet certain death. Every week or two, he would read a new passage. He was reading the stories of Evergreen.

Samira whispered when they lay side by side one night, "You need to tell the story."

"I've been telling you every detail all along," he said.

"Not to me," she whispered. "You need to tell it to the world."

"You think so?" He said.

"You need to tell the story," she said as she drifted asleep.

He pulled his chair up to the desk. He took another sip of bourbon and centered the keyboard before him.

He began to type. His fingers danced across the keys...

Billy Blaine first saw the small door in his basement during the summer of 1962...

WE HOPE YOU ENJOYED THE STORIES OF EVERGREEN TRILOGY

IF THIS WAS YOUR FIRST STEP INTO EVERGREEN, WE'D LOVE FOR YOU TO SEE HOW IT ALL BEGAN!

VC